I,
Lorelei

By
Yeardley Smith

Laura Geringer Books
An Imprint of HarperCollinsPublishers

Library of Congress Cataloging-in-Publication Data
Smith, Yeardley.
I, Lorelei / by Yeardley Smith. — 1st ed.
    p.   cm.
Summary: In letters to her recently deceased cat Mud, eleven-year-old Lorelei chronicles
the ups and downs of her sixth-grade year, during which her parents separate, she gets a
part in the school play, and she becomes friends with the cutest boy in her grade.
ISBN 978-0-06-149344-7 (trade bdg.) — ISBN 978-0-06-149345-4 (lib. bdg.)
[1. Divorce—Fiction.   2. Family life—Washington (D.C.)—Fiction.   3. Schools—
Fiction.   4. Interpersonal relations—Fiction.   5. Cats—Fiction.   6. Letters—Fiction.
7. Washington (D.C.)—Fiction.]   I. Title.
PZ7.S6632Ial   2009   2008007291
[Fic]—dc22   CIP
                                                                                AC

Typography by Carla Weise
1   2   3   4   5   6   7   8   9   10
❖
First Edition

For Clementine

This Diary Belongs to
LORELEI LEE CONNELLY.

◎

If you find it, please mind your
own business and DO NOT READ.
Then mail it to:
742 Albemarle Street NW,
Washington, DC 20016
Thank you.

◎

Both this diary and the story of
my life are dedicated to Mud:
a great listener.

Dear Mud,

I've decided to start keeping a diary, so that when I become a famous writer/actress/chef I'll remember everything that happened to me. Plus, when I'm dead, and someone wants to write my biography, they won't have to make stuff up about me.

All right, here goes. My first official entry.

My name is Lorelei, and today I'm 4,126 days old. That's 11¼ years. Also, I'm a Cancer the Crab, if you follow astrology like I do.

I have brown hair, which is mostly straight and down to my shoulders. But I've been putting egg yolks and olive oil on it for the past two weeks to make it grow faster, and I can already tell it's working. My eyes are blue and I had twenty-seven freckles at last count.

My mom's name is Claire. My dad's is Theo. And I have two smelly brothers—one older and one younger.

1

Teddy is fourteen and Ryan is the runt, age four.

My English teacher, Miss Dove, says that a lot of writers picture someone in their mind when they write. She says it makes them feel like they're having a conversation. Since you and I used to talk all the time, Mud, I've decided to picture you. Cause even though you're a cat and you're dead now, you were an excellent listener when you were alive.

Miss Dove also said writers need their own space—that's why I'm writing to you from the attic. I found a nice comfy chair and a little table that doesn't rock too much when I lean on it. I put them by the window so I can look out at the garden and see your grave under the giant maple tree.

I hope you liked the funeral we had for you today. It was hard to know what to say on such short notice.

Hey, the vase I left by your grave fell over and the blue carnations are lying in the dirt! Don't worry. I'm going downstairs right now to fix it.

I miss you terribly, Mud. I still remember what you smelled like and I miss that, too.

Love,

Lorelei xo

Dear Mud,

How does it feel to be dead? Surely by now you've reached Heaven, which means you probably don't feel like a twenty-year-old cat with arthritis and kidney problems anymore. You probably feel great. All thawed out and everything.

About that: I'm sorry Mom put your body in the freezer! She was terribly upset when she found you dead by the hydrangeas. It was late, and she thought we should wait until morning to have your funeral. It was my idea to wrap you in a blanket, at least.

So what do you do all day in Heaven? Is it like camp? Do the cats get along with the dogs? Do you have your own cloud?

I bet our neighborhood looks friendly from way up there. Like a really cool model town with winding streets and alleys, and tall, slender brick houses pressed together

3

in copycat rows. I've always been glad we live on a corner, cause at least we only have neighbors looking into our backyard from one side.

I bet the giant elm trees look amazing too, all of them bursting with red and yellow leaves. Remember the day you got stuck in the one in our front yard and we had to call the fire department to get you down? You were almost too high for the fireman to reach you!

I hope you're happy in Heaven, Mud. I hope there are sunny walkways for you to lie on like there were down here. I always knew where to find you when the weather was good. In the mornings you'd trot across the street and stretch out on the Lotts' brick wall to soak up the sun. And in the late afternoon you'd be curled up under the maple in our backyard. That's why I thought it'd be the perfect place to bury you.

Hey, who's going to walk me to and from the store from now on, when Mom sends me for milk? She could never believe how you'd just stop and wait for me at the corner of Wisconsin Avenue until I got back.

"How does he know you'll only be gone a few minutes?" she'd say, shaking her head in disbelief.

"He's a cat. He knows everything," I'd tell her.

Green Bean (our other cat—for you biographers) keeps looking under the living room curtains and in the linen

4

closet for you. She's also been sniffing the blanket you used to share with her at the bottom of my bookcase and howling. I tried to explain to her you're not coming back, but she doesn't want to hear it. She just stares at the book-case and howls.

Earlier this afternoon, I picked her up, got into bed, and pulled the covers over us, to see if that would make her feel better. Didn't.

Since I'm documenting my life, I'm going to paste what I wrote for your funeral below, so you'll never forget how much I love you and wish you were still here.

Ode to Mud
By Lorelei Lee Connelly

Even though most people in the world didn't meet you, I bet they wish they had, cause you were the best cat ever. I can't believe you're gone. Today when I went to feed Green Bean, I got a bowl out for you, too, and then I remembered.

Mom likes to remind me that my first word as a baby was "Mud." She says she'll never forget the day she found you. Someone had put you in a mailbox outside her college dorm. You were so dirty, she named you Mud.

We're all going to miss seeing you sleeping under

the Christmas tree this year. And we're going to miss watching cartoons with you on Saturday mornings too. We'll even miss the dead birds you used to leave for us on the doorstep. We know you meant them as presents.

Did you know you were nine years old when I was born? That means I've known you all my life.

Oh, Mud, there's so much I want to say. I thought yesterday, the day you died, was the saddest day of my life. But today is no better. I think a piece of me will be sad forever.

I would give anything if you could come back for just one more visit, Mud. Anything. I will never forget you.

Love always and forever,

Lorelei

Ugh.

I can't believe it—the wind knocked your vase over again!

Love,

Lorelei

DAILY HOROSCOPE FOR
CANCER THE CRAB:
It's a perfect time to be assertive
and move forward in your career.
Seize the day.

Dear Mud,

That's pretty good news, don't you think? Well, it would be if I had a job. I wonder if just being eleven could be considered a job. I mean, it sucks up all my time and extra thinking. Isn't that what a job does?

It's only been two days since we buried you, and already Teddy is saying, "Life goes on."

But how? I cried in the girls' bathroom after my math and gym classes, cause I miss you more today than I did yesterday. I didn't even think that was possible.

Yesterday Mom was sobbing right alongside me, and today she was completely fine. I don't get it. But she's always been like that. Like a robot: On. Off. On. Off.

For the past two weeks, I've been practicing my audition song for the middle school play by singing in the shower. Sometimes I don't even turn the water on—I just stand in the tub, shoes and all, and belt out "Tomorrow," from *Annie*, until my lungs shrivel up like raisins.

FYI, all you biographers, I'm a sixth grader at Pinkerton, and the middle school always does a musical in the fall.

Pinkerton's a private school in Washington, DC, with grades from kindergarten through twelve, all on the same campus, but in separate buildings.

The lower school is at one end of campus. The middle school is crammed in next to the athletic field. And the upper school is in the two new buildings on campus with the gymnasium and auditorium in them, which are open to all grades.

Even though it's a private school, Pinkerton's not half as snotty as National Cathedral School, or Sidwell Friends. They're snotty with a capital S! Although I suppose if you beat us in sports every time, you might be stuck on yourself too.

Auditions for the middle school play are tomorrow afternoon, and we're doing a musical version of *Peter Pan*. At first, I thought it'd be fun to play Wendy. Until last week when Mom sat me down and said, "Lorelei, I heard they're doing *Peter Pan* at your school this year." (As if I didn't know.) "I think you should try out for Wendy."

Turns out she played Wendy at Princeton University.

Figures. She says she got a standing ovation every night, and that the local paper gave her a wonderful review, saying she showed real promise.

"What happened?" I asked.

"Oh, you know. . . ." My mother blushed and looked away.

"No. Do you mean you didn't really want to be an actress?"

"Well, of course I did!" she said. "I dreamed of moving to Hollywood and becoming a star, like every girl does. But Mother and Dad said I was being silly. They said I needed something to fall back on, so I finished college. And then I met your father and we got married and had you kids, and now . . . here we are." She half smiled, and her eyes got kind of watery.

A split second later, she snapped out of it and danced around me like a Gypsy, singing one of Wendy's solos.

Oh, brother. I didn't know where to look. So every time she got close to me, I just stared at her ear, which turned bright pink when she hit the high notes. Or almost hit them. I guess she's kind of out of practice.

Then she told me to sit tight while she hurried up to the attic to get her *Peter Pan* scrapbook from college. A whole scrapbook, Mud!

"I had the time of my life," she said as she flipped

through the book, smiling her sad smile. (Remember that smile?) "So you just *have* to get the part, Lorelei, because everyone wants to be Wendy. We can start a tradition: Connelly mothers and daughters starring in *Peter Pan*."

Okay, for starters it's called *PETER Pan* not *WENDY Pan*! And why does she always want me to be exactly like her?

That's when I started to think I'd rather play Tinker Bell instead of Wendy. And that my horoscope must have said "be assertive" today cause I'm supposed to march right up to my mother, tell her how I feel, and nip this whole be-like-me thing in the bud.

⊘⊘

Thirteen minutes later:

Well, I tried. But when I opened my mouth to speak, she swallowed me up in a huge hug and told me how proud of me she is. She looked so happy, I didn't know how to tell her.

A few minutes later my dad came home from work (late, as usual) and Mom started singing the Wendy song for *him*. She even tried to get him to sing the chorus with her.

"Claire, please. I'm dead tired," he groaned, and slumped onto the sofa.

"You're always tired," my mother complained.

"Well, someone has to earn the money if you're going to shop all day," my father grumbled, rubbing his face.

"Oh, now it's my fault that you got a promotion and work all the time."

"No, I'm not saying that. Look, I just want a beer and a moment to catch my breath."

"Hmmph," my mother snorted.

I hate it when they argue, Mud. And they seem to do it all the time now. So I snuck off to my room.

Oh, Mud, what am I going to do about this Wendy thing? Ugh.

Love,

Lorelei

P.S. Dad just came up to say good night.

"Has your mother been singing that song to you all day?" he asked.

I nodded. He sighed.

"Has she shown you her *Peter Pan* scrapbook from Princeton?"

I nodded again. He shook his head and chuckled.

"You know, whatever part you get, Peanut, it's okay with me. Don't you worry a fig about that. I'll handle your mother too. You just do your thing and be great, as always."

I smiled and thanked him.

"You missed Mud's funeral on Sunday," I said.

My father stroked my hair. "I know. I'm so sorry about that."

"I wish he hadn't had to die," I said, tearing up.

"I know, Peanut. But think of it this way: He had a fantastic life with us, and the time had simply come when his spirit was needed elsewhere."

"But why? Why?" I sobbed into my dad's chest.

He didn't have an answer. But he held me tight and stroked my hair for a long time, until the tears stopped coming.

I miss you, Mud. I miss you more than I've ever missed anyone in my whole life.

Love,

Lorelei xo

DAILY HOROSCOPE FOR
CANCER THE CRAB:
Your love life kicks into high gear.
Some of you singles will be
married by May.

As you can see, today's horoscope is useless, since, at age eleven, I don't have a love life. But even if I did, I don't want to get married. Not if being married puts you in a bad mood every day like my parents.

See, I bet they wouldn't get on each other's nerves as much if they were just friends, and lived in separate houses, and only saw each other five days a week like me and Jenny. Anyway . . .

Oh dear. All the talk about me auditioning for Wendy has pushed my mother over the edge. She tried to make me breakfast this morning, Mud. Yikes! You know what a bad cook she is. Even Green Bean, who loves *all* people food, won't eat my mom's cooking.

When I went downstairs, Gunda was sitting at the breakfast table, watching my mother scramble a pile of eggs and burn bacon in a pan.

For all you biographers, Gunda has been our house-keeper and nanny since my brother, Teddy, was born. She's from Norway, and get this: She used to be my *dad's* nanny when he was a boy. That's right. She's very old. At least sixty. Of course, my dad loves her to pieces. So when he got married and had his own family, he asked her to come take care of us.

When I walked into the kitchen, Mom was burning breakfast on the stove and my little brother, Ryan, was spreading his oatmeal on the comics.

"Lulu! Looky, looky!" he hollered when he saw me. He calls me Lulu; so does Gunda sometimes, cause Lorelei is too much of a mouthful for both of them, I guess.

"Wow, squirt, that's an awesome mess," I said, looking at his goopy work of art.

Teddy was asleep sitting up in a kitchen chair, chin on his chest. I shook my head.

For weeks now, Teddy has refused to take his green down jacket off when he's inside. I'm serious—he wears it *all the time*. Breakfast, lunch, dinner. I bet he sleeps in it, even.

Mom intercepted me at the fridge and practically squeezed me to death. "There's my little star! Sit down—I made you breakfast," she said, like today is Sunday and I have all the time in the world.

"But Mom, I'll be late if I don't leave right now," I said sweetly. I really didn't want to eat her cooking, but I also didn't want to hurt her feelings.

So she started frantically opening the cupboards, one after the other.

"Well, what can you take with you? A Pop-Tart? You still eat Pop-Tarts, don't you?" she asked.

My dad came into the kitchen looking handsome, as usual, in his dark-blue suit with perfectly pleated trousers and a white shirt that made him look like he had a tan. He asked my mother why she was banging cupboards.

"I'm looking for the Pop-Tarts," she said. Gunda rolled her eyes, got up, pulled three boxes of them from behind the cereal, and offered them to me.

I chose strawberry, as the bacon on the stove began to smoke.

My dad took a sip of coffee and kissed me on the head. "Good luck on your audition today," he said quietly.

"It's tomorrow," I whispered, hoping my mother hadn't heard. But she had, naturally. My mother has better hearing than a bat.

"Our little girl is going to be the next Wendy," Mom said with that spazzed-out look in her eyes.

"Well, whenever it is, just have fun. You'll be great," my father said.

15

"Will you be home in time for dinner, Theo?" Mom asked.

He nodded.

Gunda and I glanced at each other quickly. My dad hasn't been home for dinner for weeks, so why does my mother keep asking him that? And why does my father keep saying yes?

I grabbed my backpack and left.

☙❧

Before you can even audition for *Peter Pan*, one of your parents has to sign a permission slip saying it's okay. And Mr. Blair, our drama teacher, was handing out the permission slips after school in the auditorium today.

When I reached the back entrance to the big brick building, I stood on my toes and looked through the windows and down the hall. The coast was clear. No Matt Newsome.

I pulled hard on the heavy red doors and slipped inside. There were a few upper school kids at their lockers on either side of the hallway. I wished there were more. I scooted down the corridor, over the shiny tiles and the big black and red painting of our school mascot, Boaz the Bull. I could see the stairway going up to the auditorium ahead of me, and I was almost there when this huge shadow snuck

16

up behind me and blocked out the light from the ceiling. The itty-bitty hairs on my arms and legs stood straight up. I knew in my gut it was Matt Newsome.

There used to be an orange cat who lived in the alley behind our house. My older brother, Teddy, called him Psycho cause he'd pick a fight with any*one* or any*thing*, and all the dogs in the neighborhood were afraid of him.

Matt Newsome is the Psycho of Pinkerton School. He ate a live goldfish right from the tank in Teddy's Living Science class. And he has a creepy way of popping out of nowhere when you least expect it. Then you're toast.

He should be in ninth grade but he was held back, so he's in eighth grade with Teddy. Which is how, as a lowly middle schooler, Matt still manages to own the upper school hallways.

"Where do you think you're going, idiot?" he said, grabbing my arm.

His voice is really deep and quiet. I could hardly hear him. And he was squeezing so hard, my fingers were starting to tingle. I'm telling you, Mud, Matt's head alone seemed to take up the whole hallway.

"I'm going to get my permission slip for *Peter Pan*," I said quietly.

"'I'm going to get my permission slip for *Peter Pan*,'" he mocked me in a squeaky voice. "You think you're so great that they're going to forget how ugly you are and let you be in the school play? What makes *you* so special, loser?"

I drew a blank. At first I couldn't think of a single thing, Mud. And then it hit me. *I have spent too many hours practicing my song in the shower to die before I get a chance to sing it.* Plus, my mother was counting on me. *Really* counting on me.

In a single breath, I blurted out, "Cause if I don't get that permission slip, then Mr. Blair won't let me audition for *Peter Pan*. And if I don't audition for *Peter Pan*, my mother will never forgive you. Yeah, *you*, and let me tell you, nobody holds a grudge like my mother. You'll spend the rest of your life on the run cause she'll come after you, which will leave me and my brothers *motherless*! And then *we'll* come after you. And when we find you, Teddy, who can't help himself when he gets all hot under the biscuit, will beat the crap out of you and you'll be nothing but pulp. Gooey pulp that lies awake every night wishing you'd just let me get my freakin' permission slip!"

I would have gone on, except I ran out of air. But I sure shut Matt Newsome up!

For a second, anyway, till he grabbed me by the shoulder in his death grip and said, "Teddy? As in Teddy Connelly?"

I nodded yes. His breath smelled like Green Bean's. Ew. Matt pulled me up to my tiptoes, and I could feel the other kids in the hall staring at us, but no one moved. No one came to my rescue! Can you believe that?

Matt bent down until his nose was a whisker away from mine and his greasy bangs tickled my face. I was afraid to breathe, Mud, but I wouldn't look away. Not for a second. I kept my eyes glued to the red, lumpy scar across his chin. Then all of a sudden he tilted his head, and I saw them: his eyes. They're blue like mine, Mud, with eyelashes thick as a rug, and there was a big bruise under his left one. All I could think was *Who in the world has the guts to sock Matt Newsome?*

He caught me staring and said, "What are you looking at?" Then he shook his head, and the black eye disappeared behind his bangs again.

"Nothing," I whispered.

"Well, today is your lucky day, idiot." He scowled. "Teddy isn't as big an ass wipe as everybody else in this school, so I'm gonna let you go. But don't ever come down this hallway again, do you hear me?"

I just nodded, cause I didn't want to get into how that was going to be impossible.

Matt squeezed my arm and cackled. "Loser," he said, then gave me a shove toward the auditorium. I ran as fast

19

as I could until I reached the top of the stairs and met up with Jenny. We got our permission slips and walked home together.

There's no way you can forget Jenny, Mud. We've been best friends since we were five, and her family—all eight of them—live diagonally across the street from us. You used to climb up that huge tree in their front yard and razz their Jack Russell terrier, Mr. Big, remember? (Hey, have you run into him up in Heaven yet?)

Anyway, what you biographers need to know about Jenny is that she's half Balinese and she's the prettiest girl I know. She's tall and thin, and has never had a single zit. Even when she wears her sloppiest jeans, she looks like she just stepped out of *Seventeen* magazine. And her long hair is so black it's almost blue. Jenny has always wanted to be a veterinarian when she grows up, and she's plenty smart enough. The only thing is, she faints at the sight of blood.

On the way home I told her about Matt Newsome. She was speechless for at least three minutes. Do you have any idea how long three minutes is? Finally, she said she would have kicked him, if it'd been her. Which never used to be like Jenny at all. She used to be sweet as cream. But she's been really cranky lately.

Come to think of it, maybe you could keep an eye on

her from Heaven. Tell God Jenny's been whaling on tree trunks with her softball bat—in case She's been too busy to notice, that is. (Well, of course God is a She. Who else could do seven million things at once?)

Hey, what's going on? Mom's throwing out your blue carnations! They're not even dead yet. Good grief.

Love,

Lorelei xox

Dear Mud,

It's lunchtime at school and I only ate half my spaghetti so I would have time to write and tell you what happened this morning.

I think my mom is losing it.

While I was taking my shower and singing "Tomorrow," she went up to the attic and got the nightie she wore as Wendy at Princeton and laid it out across my bed. It's flannel with little blue flowers and a lacy white collar. Does she seriously think I'm going to wear it to my audition? You couldn't pay me to wear a nightie like that! And it smells like musty old mothballs to boot.

She wrote a note in red crayon and pinned it to the collar: BREAK A LEG, MY LITTLE WENDY, with a big, sloppy heart around it. As soon as I saw it, I got a big knot in my stomach.

When I went downstairs to the kitchen, she was waiting for me. She was in her bathrobe and her hair looked pretty piggy but, as usual, her lipstick was perfect.

Gunda was sitting at the little kitchen table again watching my mother make breakfast. Today it was oatmeal.

The entire box of oatmeal, which raises so many questions. The most important one being How come my mother doesn't know I hate oatmeal?! It makes me fart like an elephant.

Anyway, she must have been cooking it for forty-five minutes, cause you could have plugged potholes with it. When she scooped it into the bowl, it was so stiff she had to pry it off the spoon with a spatula.

I made myself take two bites cause I didn't want to hurt her feelings, but it was gross, Mud. I asked if I could have a Pop-Tart instead. And do you know what she said?

"Whatever you like, my little Wendy."

The knot in my stomach doubled. I couldn't even eat my Pop-Tart.

"Did you see I put my Wendy nightie on your bed?" she asked.

"Yes."

"I thought you'd like to take it to school with you. Maybe wear it for your audition for good luck."

"Oh . . . No, thank you," I said politely.

"Are you sure?" My mother smiled, and got that spazzed-out look in her eyes.

"Yup, I'm sure," I answered, and zipped out the door.

Mud, don't you think it's odd she doesn't see how much pressure she's putting on me with this Wendy thing? Good grief, it's a wonder I went to school today at all. A person with less character would have passed out or pretended to have appendicitis, or something, just so they could have gotten out of auditioning altogether.

But I want to make my mom proud. I do, Mud. Even if it may be practically impossible.

More later.

⊙⁄⊙

7:46 P.M.

I'm in the attic now, looking out the window at the way the back porch light shines perfectly on the circle of stones I placed on your grave today. Jenny got a statue of a dog carrying a bone for Mr. Big's grave when he died. So I told Mom you deserve a better marker than a bunch of rocks, and she said we can get something this weekend.

Oh, I have heaps to tell you. Wait until you hear what happened at *Peter Pan* auditions.

I was a couple of minutes late since I took the long way

to the auditorium today and went in the front entrance. I didn't want to waste time running into Matt Newsome again. I had bigger fish to fry.

Inside the auditorium, Mr. Blair, our drama teacher and director, was already giving a speech, so I slipped into a seat in the back row that Jenny was saving for me.

Did I tell you Mr. Blair only has one arm? No kidding. Some people say he lost the other one in a boating accident while he was deep-sea fishing. Like a shark ate it. But then you have to wonder why the shark didn't eat the rest of him, too.

Jenny heard another story from Veronica, who heard it from Neely, who heard it from her brother, that Mr. Blair's missing arm got sucked off in a swimming pool filter. Now that seems more like it. Mr. Blair doesn't look like the type of person who'd ever leave the beach, let alone go deep-sea fishing.

When I snuck in, he was in the middle of saying, "If you didn't bring a song, you can sing 'Happy Birthday.' We may also ask you to read a scene from the play, which we have copies of right here," he explained, holding up a wad of papers in his left hand while his empty right sleeve hung like a flag, perfectly folded and pinned to itself about where his elbow would have been. "I think you'll find we've done a marvelous adaptation of the play for our middle school production. By the same token, if we do not ask you to read a scene from the play, it does not mean you didn't get a part. It just means we don't need to hear you read," Mr. Blair said.

He always refers to himself as "we."

"Let's get started. And remember to sing with your soul, people." With that, Mr. Blair put his hand on his hip and called Andy Butterfield to the stage.

All you need to know about Andy is that she's a seventh grader and thinks she's Queen of Everything.

She sang "God Bless America," and it stank. You probably heard it up in Heaven and thought, "What the heck is *that*?"

Of course, *she* thought it was perfect and took six bows, even though everyone stopped clapping after one.

Next was Drew Pembroke, one of only four boys who showed up for auditions today. If Drew were a thing, he'd be a pipe cleaner, cause he's tall, with bushy black hair, and kind of pinky-orange. He's so skinny that when he turns sideways, all you can see is his nose sticking out over his top lip. He has a good voice, though. Really deep. *And* he's done community theater, so people say he's going places.

But not today.

Today he cracked in the middle of his song, which was

"Yesterday" by the Beatles, and he nearly passed out from embarrassment. His face went from pinky-orange to red, to purple.

The thing is, even though his voice cracked and he forgot the words to one whole verse, you can tell he's an incredible singer. So it was no surprise Mr. Blair asked him to read the part of Captain Hook, which I thought was a really good sign. Unfortunately, Drew was a nervous wreck by then, and he couldn't get his hands to stop shaking, which made him lose his place in the scene—twice! Ooof! It was like watching a fly trapped in a jar.

Mr. Blair called on Saylor Creek next. I hadn't even noticed she was at auditions, which is sort of the sad thing with Saylor: Nobody ever notices she's anywhere, even though she's huge and it should be impossible to miss her. But she just seems to blend in with the wall.

Poor Saylor. I've been in the same class with her since kindergarten, and I don't remember her ever having a single friend, which has made her pretty mean. So now, even if someone wanted to be her friend, I doubt she'd let them.

As she waddled to the stairs and climbed onto the stage, someone did an armpit fart. I didn't think it was funny, but the other kids laughed. Mr. Blair turned around and shushed us. Saylor's so used to it, she didn't even look up. Just kept on walking. Oh, Mud, it made the backs of my knees sweat and my mouth dry up so much, I felt like I was sucking on a mitten. I just wanted her to be great. I wanted her to win for once.

But she sure doesn't make it easy on herself. The giant yellow sweatshirt she was wearing had an old ketchup stain on it, and it could have doubled as a pup tent. Then there's her stringy blond hair, her pimples, and the wall-eye. Not to mention she spits when she talks.

Saylor stood center stage, looking over our heads. People giggled. She gave the bottom of her sweatshirt a tug.

"I'm going to sing 'Somewhere over the Rainbow,'" she said, to no one in particular, in a voice deep enough to be my dad's.

What happened next was nothing short of amazing. Saylor Creek opened her mouth and sang perfectly. Just like an angel. I had goose bumps all over.

I looked at Jenny. Her face said the same thing as mine: *How is Saylor doing that?* Cause it doesn't make any sense. I'm telling you, Mud, Saylor has sounded like a truck driver since kindergarten. So where did she learn to sing like Judy Garland?

When she finished, no one could speak. All they could do was clap. And clap. And clap! A cheer even went up on the athletic field, which made it seem like the whole school was congratulating Saylor, and she actually smiled. At least I think that was a smile.

The thing I can't figure out is why Mr. Blair didn't ask her to read the part of Wendy. All he said was "Thank you, Saylor," and let her go back to her seat.

I wanted to leap up and say, "Wait a minute! You *have* to let her read for Wendy." But I didn't. I chickened out like a gutless lame-o.

Of course, God immediately punished me for being yellow-bellied and made me audition next.

I should have explained to Mr. Blair, calmly, that it's totally unfair to ask me to follow Saylor. She's a billion times better than me. But like I said, God had me for being gutless.

In a split second, the horror of it all dawned on me, Mud. Escaping Matt Newsome was easy-peasy. Singing in public was going to be the death of me. You know, for all my mother's encouragement, she could have given me some emergency pointers, too!

I dragged my butt down the aisle and up the stairs to center stage. I could feel everyone's eyes on my back, and it made me antsy. But I took a deep breath and started to sing.

"The sun'll come out tomorrow—"

Oh, no, I started too high! I heard myself yell in my head. Eeeep! *Too high!* I died inside! Died, I tell you!

I knew if I continued in that key, I would never make it through the song without cracking and losing it, just like Drew Pembroke. Only if I didn't make it through my song, my life was as good as over. How would I ever be able to go home and face my mother?

Suddenly I heard myself say out loud, "I'd like to start over, please."

"Okay, take your time," said Mr. Blair, and crossed his arm over his chest, calm as you please.

The thing is, I was eerily calm too. I sang quietly to myself for a second, found my key, and started again.

From the first note I sang to the last, the song soared out of me. It was magic, Mud. Magic.

Afterward, I opened my eyes to see Jenny and everybody smiling and clapping. Mr. Blair said, "Very good, Lorelei. Thank you. Would you look at the part of Tiger Lily, please?"

It wasn't exactly what I was going for, but I didn't care. I was just happy to live another day.

Next Mr. Blair called on Jenny. She sang "Memory" from the musical *Cats*. She did a good job. Didn't even seem nervous, except for her hands balled into fists at her sides.

Afterward Mr. Blair asked her to read for the part of Wendy. Figures. *Everybody* likes Jenny. And if Saylor

Creek hadn't just blown us all away with "Over the Rainbow," I'd say Jenny would get Wendy for sure, but nobody could beat Saylor. Plus, Jenny read the part with a Southern accent like Scarlett O'Hara from *Gone with the Wind*. I'm still trying to figure out why Mr. Blair didn't say anything about that. But he just patted her on the back and said, "That was remarkable, Jenny."

I'm telling you, Jenny could sell wet to water.

Crumb, it's getting late and I still have to study my French. I'll just give you the highlights of the other auditions.

The Ferry twins did a duet. No words, just "Bong, bong, bong," like they were bells. They were really good. Jenny and I think they should do sound effects for the play.

Short and shaggy Curley Portis, the sixth-grade class clown, was next. He sang this song called "Let's Call the Whole Thing Off" about a potato and a "poe-tah-toe," a tomato and a "toe-mah-toe." And he did a jig to go with it. It was pretty funny.

Veronica Stavros, who was squeezed into a cheerleader outfit that was tight enough you could see where her bellybutton dents in, sang "My Heart Belongs to Daddy" like she was an upper schooler. All slithery, and flirty, and breathy like a dingbat. She thinks just cause she's the first girl in our class to get boobs, everyone wants to see them. Boring.

I really have to go, but I have to tell you about Paul Windsor. Paul skipped a grade a few years back, so he's an eighth grader now. But he's small for his age, with a high voice. I don't need to tell you, he gets teased *a lot*.

Anyway, he sang Rolf's verse in "Sixteen Going on Seventeen" from *The Sound of Music*, spinning and twirling around the stage just like they do in the movie. It was brilliant. He was so light on his feet.

He should have gotten huge applause. But apart from me and Jenny, Mr. Blair was the only other person who clapped—or slapped. Hard to clap with only one hand. Not that Mr. Blair lets that stop him. He just goes right ahead and slaps his leg. *Slappity! Slappity! Slap!*

Of course, he asked Paul to read the part of Peter Pan. After which, Mr. Blair slapped some more and said Paul did it just like Cathy Rigby, his favorite Peter of all time. (I know, a girl playing Peter Pan? I don't get it.)

Well, when Paul heard the name Cathy Rigby, he went from really happy to *really* mad in about one second, and looked like he was going to cry. I couldn't watch. I pretended to be tying my shoe as he walked back to his seat, cause I thought if I concentrated on something other than his face, such as my sneaker, I could *will* him not to cry.

It kind of worked. His face turned red, but I didn't see any tears when he sat down across the aisle from me. Still, I doubt that kept him from getting beat up on his way home from school today, cause that just seems to be his lot in life.

There were more auditions too, but those are the highlights.

Ugh. Mom and Dad are out and Teddy's yelling that Mom's on the phone and I have to talk to her.

☙❧

Six minutes later:

I'm back. Mom and Dad are at some charity dinner in Richmond, Virginia, tonight, and won't be home until late. But Mom had to call and see how my audition went.

I told her it was pretty good.

"Tell me every little thing," she said.

But I didn't start with me—I started with Saylor, and how she sang so beautifully everyone was speechless. A few minutes later I realized we'd been cut off, which means the rest will have to wait. Fine by me.

Thanks for listening today, Mud. Green Bean is still really down. She's not crying in front of the bookcase anymore, but now she'll hardly come out of my closet. And she's not eating very much. Mom says she's in mourning.

It hurts my heart to see her like that.

I told Jenny she should write to Mr. Big like I write to you, cause he died two years ago and she still misses him every day. But she thinks she waited too long and he won't be able to hear her now. I said I was sure that's not true. So maybe she'll try.

Hugs and smooches,

Lorelei xoxo

Dear Mud,

It's only 5:20 in the morning and already I've been up for hours.

My parents got home from their charity thing in Richmond at around 3:30 A.M. I wouldn't even know that, except Mom came into my room and sat on the edge of my bed and stared at me.

How do I know, if I was sleeping? you ask.

Cause I could *feel* her. The same as when Jenny and I are passing notes in math class and suddenly, without even looking, we can *feel* Ms. Kurtz (aka The Water Buffalo) staring at us and we know we're busted.

"Mom, what are you doing?" I yawned as I sat up and rubbed my eyes.

"Oh, I'm sorry, sweetie. I just wanted to come in and look at my little star."

She turned on the light and said now that I was up, she

would love to hear how everything went.

I couldn't help wondering why she doesn't care this much about my grades. But when she gave me a big hug, and held on really tight, like she'd been waiting all day to see me, I forgot about being annoyed with her.

Even at 3:30 in the morning, my mother smelled sweet and looked fresh and beautiful in her black dress, high heels, and soft pink lipstick. Her hair was in a loose twist just above her neck. Was she always like that, Mud? Sweet smelling and lovely? Even when you were a kitten?

I was just happy she wasn't running around doing a thousand other things. For once my mother was perfectly still and I had her all to myself. I can't remember the last time that happened. Not since Ryan was born, anyway.

I tucked myself into her. Tried to make myself as small and quiet as possible, and held on as long as she would let me. (Not very long.)

She sat me up with that wild look in her eyes. "Well, how did it go? How did you do? Are you going to be Pinkerton Middle School's next Wendy?"

I couldn't get a word in.

She rushed on, "Did you tell Mr. Blair that *I* played Wendy in college and if he gives you the part you already have a costume?

"You know, I saved all my music from that production too, so I can teach you the songs. Oh, Lorelei, this is thrilling! Wait until I tell your father's aunt Lee that the Connelly women are starting a new tradition. When do you start rehearsals? Maybe I can come and just be a fly on the wall for a few of them. Wouldn't that be fun? I could give you some pointers."

"*Mom!*" I yelled. She was so startled, she almost slid off the bed.

Tears started to dribble off my chin. "You're driving me crazy! I'm not going to get Wendy, okay? Quit bugging me about it!"

"I'm sorry. I'll leave you alone," she whispered, and got up to go.

"No, don't," I said, cause she had it all wrong. I didn't want her to go. I wanted her to hug me, and just understand. Why can't she understand, Mud? "Don't go," I pleaded, slurping up tears.

She looked at me, then carefully sat at the end of my bed.

My dad poked his head in the doorway to see what all the noise was about.

"Everything all right?" he asked.

Mom nodded, but I shook my head.

"Well, at least you're in agreement." He chuckled.

"It's not funny," I said.

He came and sat between us and put his arm around my shoulders.

"Girls, girls," he sighed. "I know I'm just the guy who puts cheese on the table. And let me be the first to admit that there's plenty I don't understand about the delicate ways mothers and daughters relate to each other. But I'm going to put my head in the walrus's mouth here, and suggest that whatever has you two all fired up will seem less like the end of civilization when the clock doesn't say three fifty-five A.M. Why don't you both get some sleep?"

I rolled my eyes.

"I know." Dad smiled. "I'm just the cheese guy. And while I can't say for sure what you two beauties are talking about, I have a pretty good idea. So let me remind you both that things will work out exactly the way they're supposed to."

My mother nodded slowly.

"And did I mention the positive effects of sleep?" he hinted again.

I half expected my mother to snap at him or give him the hairy eyeball, since everything he says seems to bug her these days. But she actually kind of smiled.

When Dad got no answer from either of us, though, he sighed, kissed us each on the cheek, and went to bed.

Mom folded her hands in her lap and stared up at the ceiling. I prepared for the worst, which is usually a lecture about how the Connellys are a little better than everybody else. Meaning we have an obligation to be exceptional every time we leave the house. And each time we aren't, it's like wiping a big green booger on the family name.

So I was gobsmacked when she gave me a hug, then held me gently at arm's length and said, "Lorelei, the secret of a satisfied life is making the most of every opportunity that comes your way. The outcome isn't nearly as important as knowing that you gave it your all. It sounds like that's exactly what you did at your audition, and I'm very proud of you."

She kissed me on the forehead.

"And I'm sorry you felt like I was bugging you. How awful!" She laughed. "I just thought it would be fun if you were Wendy."

I hugged her tightly. Then she tucked me in and left.

I haven't been able get back to sleep since, cause I keep trying to figure out *Who kidnapped my mother?*

Do you think she'll remember she said all those things when she wakes up later this morning?

Your gobsmacked pal,

Lorelei

I think this is the longest day of my life. It's still Friday the 21st. And boy, do I have a story for you!

Everyone in my class has to put together a time capsule for social studies class. So I was up in the attic looking for stuff to put in mine. I was digging through that beat-up leather trunk with the metal corners that Mom keeps our family memories in. Stuff like our baby clothes, yearbooks, photographs, tennis trophies from college, and her Dairy Princess Crown from high school. (I love that thing!)

And way at the bottom I see this old *Us Magazine* with that actress Gretchen Terra on the cover.

Why would you save this? I wondered.

Inside were pictures of Gretchen walking her Saint Bernard, Willow; getting her car washed; and going to parties. Blah, blah, blah.

Then there was a photo of Gretchen at a charity ball holding hands with a guy who looked just like my dad. I looked closer. Mud, it *was* my dad!

I couldn't believe it! I brought the magazine right up to my nose to get a better look and read the caption under the photo once, twice, three times: "Gretchen gets cozy with old flame Theodore Merritt Connelly III. Can you say romance?"

Do you know what this means, Mud? I AM THE DAUGHTER OF A DAD WHO DATED A MOVIE STAR!

Which explains why, when I was brushing my teeth tonight and looked in the mirror, I noticed my eyes were shining like sparklers on the Fourth of July and I looked noticeably taller.

It makes me smile, Mud.

I've stashed the magazine under my mattress for now. Jenny and I are hanging out tomorrow, and I can't wait to show her, even though she'll probably notice the glow about me before I even say anything.

Did I ever tell you that before my grandpa died last summer, we used to play this game? He would say, "Lorelei, if you could relive seven days of your life, which would they be?" Then he'd give me sixty seconds to decide.

And I'd just laugh and laugh cause I could never decide. I always wanted to take the morning from Tuesday, and the afternoon from some Saturday, and suppertime from a Thursday, and piece together a whole new day. And that's as far as I'd get.

Grandpa would chuckle and call me a cheater, then tell me *his* seven days. I can't remember them all, but I remember a few, like the day he got married; the days my mom and her brother, Augie, were born; the first time somebody called him *Dr.* Clemmons; and the day he discovered Boston cream pie.

Well, Mud, if you see him, please tell Grandpa that today would be one of my reliving days. I'll take the whole thing: from mom waking me up at 3:30 this morning to the hamburgers with real Wonder Bread buns we got to have for dinner to discovering that I, Lorelei Lee Connelly, am the daughter of a father who dated a movie star.

Wow, what a day!

Love,

Lorelei xxx

Sunday, October 23rd

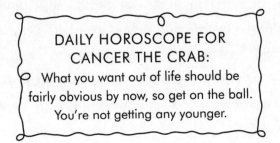

DAILY HOROSCOPE FOR
CANCER THE CRAB:
What you want out of life should be
fairly obvious by now, so get on the ball.
You're not getting any younger.

Dear Mud,

I thought your horoscope was supposed to help you figure out what to do each day. But mine's never any help and it's really bossy. How the heck am I supposed to know what I want out of life? I'm eleven. Gee whiz.

When I got up early this morning, I ran downstairs to show my dad the *Us* magazine, but Gunda said he'd gone in to work.

"Again? But it's Sunday." I sighed.

Gunda put her finger to her lips. "Sssshhhh. Your mother doesn't know yet. Maybe she wake up in good mood and not notice."

"Very funny," I said.

Ever since Dad became a partner at the law firm, he's been working a lot of Sundays, and having dinner at the office almost every night of the week. In the beginning

43

Mom was really proud of him. She would go down to the office a couple of nights a week and eat with him. But Teddy says he overheard Dad say she had to stop coming, which made her mad, and now she accuses Dad of being more in love with his job than he is with his family.

"You want some pancakes?" Gunda said. "I make for your brothers."

"No thanks. I'm not that hungry. Hey, Gunda, look at this," I said, and showed her the *Us* magazine.

She smacked her forehead with her hand, "Oh no, where you find dat thing, Kylling?" (That's Gunda's special nickname for me. It means "chicken" in Norwegian.)

"I found it in the attic. I'm going to put it in my time capsule for social studies."

"No. I tell you, run and put in garbage. Go now."

"Why?"

"Why what?" my mother said, coming into the kitchen in her robe, Ryan trailing behind her.

I slapped the Sunday comics over the magazine to hide it. "Why is Teddy such a jerk?" I said, pretending to be all hot under the biscuit.

"Don't talk that way about your brother, Lorelei," my mother gently scolded.

Gunda shot me a look like, *Quick thinking, Kylling.*

"Well, I'm going to Jenny's." I grabbed my coat and slipped out the back door with the magazine under my sweater.

Before I even reached Jenny's front yard, I could hear Jinger and Juliet, Jenny's twin sisters, shrieking and arguing. "It's my turn!" "Nuh-uh, it's my turn!"

In case you're wondering, Mud, nothing has changed. Jenny's house is still the loudest one on the block. (For you biographers, the Owenses only have three bedrooms and there are *eight* people living there!) Poor Jenny never has a moment of privacy unless she goes outside or to a friend's. Which she tries to do whenever possible cause as long as she's home, she's expected to help cook, or clean, or babysit her five sisters: June (who's 8), January (5), Jinger and Juliet (4), and Jasmine (2½). Her parents went a little overboard with the Js, don't you think?

As I went through the low garden gate, Jinger and Juliet tore past the big picture window in the living room with January right behind them, screaming at the top of her lungs. Seconds later Mrs. Owens sprinted by. She's fast, but she'll never catch them, cause Jinger, Juliet, and January are way faster.

As soon as I reached the front door, there was a giant *crash!* inside the house, and the girls' squeals and laughter instantly turned to heaving sobs.

Mrs. Owens shouted over them, "Well, I've told you a hundred times not to run in the house. Junior, can you help me, please?"

I always thought it was funny that Jenny's father's name was Junior, cause it's not short for anything. It's just Junior Owens, like his parents forgot to name the rest of him.

I knocked on the door. Instead of answering it, Mrs. Owens pushed open the mail slot and huffed, "Who is it?"

I bent down. "It's Lorelei. Can Jenny come out and play?"

Mrs. Owens didn't answer, but the mail slot clapped shut, which meant Jenny would be out in a minute.

I sat on the swing set in their front yard and waited. Jenny burst through the door and leaped down the steps.

"Come on. Let's go," she said quickly.

We skedaddled down the sidewalk just as Mrs. Owens yelled after us, "Jenny, take June with you!"

But we took off around the corner, toward the park, like we hadn't heard her.

We found a bench half hidden behind a tree, away from everybody, and plopped down to catch our breath. I laid the *Us* magazine beside me and turned to Jenny.

"Are you okay?" I said.

Jenny shook her head. "My mother's pregnant again."

"Not again!" I gasped.

Jenny nodded. "She and Dad are sure this one's going to be a boy." She rolled her eyes.

"Yeesh."

"I know. I told my parents if they have any more kids after this, I'm leaving."

"What did they say?"

"They laughed. But I'm serious, Lorelei. I don't know where I'd go, but I'll go."

"No wonder you've been mucho crabby lately."

"Who says I've been crabby?" She scowled, like I'd just called her a bad word.

"Nobody. Sorry, forget it. . . . Hey, look at this," I said, changing the subject. I showed her the magazine and turned to the picture of my dad and Gretchen. "My dad dated a movie star. Isn't that cool?"

"Where'd you get this?" Jenny asked, not smiling.

"I found it in an old trunk in the attic. I'm going to put it in my time capsule for social studies."

Jenny looked at the cover, then back at the photo of my dad and Gretchen, and said, "Sometimes you're so stuck-up, Lorelei."

I laughed cause I thought she was kidding, Mud. I really did. But she wasn't.

She slapped the magazine down between us. "Just because your dad dated a movie star doesn't make *you* special. I mean, it's not like he *married* her or anything. Have you ever even met Gretchen Terra? Of course not. So I don't know why you think this makes *you* so great."

Oh, brother! But this is the way it's been with Jenny for months. You never know what's coming.

"Never mind," I said to her. "I just thought it was cool, that's all. You don't have to agree if you don't want to."

"I'm just saying, you shouldn't show this to everybody, because they'll think you're bragging," said Jenny.

Now I was mad. "Big whoop. You brag all the time."

"Well, how do you think your mom would feel if she knew you were bragging about a picture of your dad with a beautiful famous actress, instead of her?"

I rolled my eyes as Jenny blabbed on. "Maybe you found it in a trunk because your parents don't want you to see it," she snapped.

"That's stupid!" I yelled.

"Why are you being such a jerk?" she yelled back.

"*Me?* I'm not being a jerk! *You're* being the—" I stopped and bit my lip. I wanted to be nice, Mud. I told myself, *Be nice. Be nice. Be nice.* I took a deep breath and started over. "I don't think the magazine was in the trunk cause my parents don't want me to see it. That's all."

"Fine, forget it." Jenny shrugged.

"Fine."

We sat in silence and I stared out at the park. It was busy today. There was a group of people throwing a Frisbee around, one lady was teaching her dog to fetch, and some guy was painting a picture of the trees all dressed up in their red and yellow leaves.

Do they have parks in Heaven, Mud? What a stupid question. They have everything in Heaven. It's Heaven! And I bet the grass stays mowed all by itself, doesn't it? Man, Teddy would love that.

Jenny started to giggle.

"What's so funny?" I said.

"You know Bo Emerson, in our class?"

"Yeah."

"I think he likes me."

This was big news. "Do you like him?" I asked, forgetting about our fight.

"Duh!" She grinned.

Bo Emerson happens to be the cutest boy in the sixth grade. Picture this: curly dark-blond hair, toffee-colored skin, and green eyes! The most amazing green eyes, Mud. Of course, he's a perfect gentleman to boot.

His mom is black and his dad is white. And none of us girls can figure out why he doesn't have a girlfriend yet.

I mean, he could date a seventh grader if he wanted to, that's how cute and popular he is.

"What makes you think he likes you?" I asked Jenny.

"I saw him staring at me in English class on Wednesday. And then he walked me to the cafeteria at lunchtime."

"Why didn't he sit with us?" I said, cause Jenny and I eat lunch together every day, and Bo has never eaten with us.

"He's probably just working up to it." She shrugged, twirling her hair around her finger.

"Yeah . . . probably." I nodded. But I don't know, Mud. I remember Wednesday. And I remember Jenny's the one who went up to *Bo* after class, and she asked *him*, "Want to walk with me to lunch?"

And Bo being Bo said, "Okay."

So does that still count as Bo liking Jenny? Or just not wanting to hurt her feelings? I need answers, Mud!

Just then Veronica Stavros came running across the park. How she saw us on that bench half hidden behind a tree, I'll never know.

Veronica's a snot. I know she doesn't like me cause whenever the three of us are together, she ignores me completely. And yet Jenny keeps inviting her to eat lunch with us and passing notes to her in English class. What gives?

"Hi, Jen!" Veronica said, waving to Jenny only. Snot.

Jenny got up and waved back. "Hey, Ronnie!"

Veronica hates being called that, but Jenny does it anyway.

I slipped the *Us* magazine under my coat.

"Hi, Ronnie," I said, just to bug her.

She gave me a dirty look.

"I'm going to the store to get some sodas for my mom and her boyfriend. Want to come?" Veronica asked Jenny.

"Sure."

I tagged along with them for a while, just to irk Veronica, but they wouldn't even make room for me on the sidewalk. So I walked behind them and put little pieces of dead grass in Ronnie's frizzy brown hair. When we reached the store, I said I had to go.

Veronica went on ahead, but Jenny turned around and waved. That's when she saw the dead grass in Veronica's hair. Her eyes went wide and I thought she was going to rat me out, for sure. But she didn't. She gave me the thumbs up and kept on walking.

Boy, Mud, today was one of those weekend days when you need a whole nother weekend just to recover from your weekend!

Mom is calling us for dinner. More later.

Love,

Lorelei oxo

> **DAILY HOROSCOPE FOR
> CANCER THE CRAB:**
> *Yikes! The planets are forecasting
> conflict, and lots of it. Avoid getting
> caught up in the drama. And don't
> worry—everyone will be feeling
> much calmer tomorrow.*

Dear Mud,

Hmmmm. . . . Considering my horoscope is pretty much always wrong about me, I'm hoping today's is a bunch of hooey also. Still, just to be on the safe side, I'd like to be a Capricorn until tomorrow. Their horoscope says: *Good things are coming. Have a nice day.* Lucky ducks.

How do you like the giant conch shell I put on your grave today? I think it's better than the rocks, and it's just for now, until my mom takes me to the garden store to get a real marker for you. She keeps promising we'll do it tomorrow. Then tomorrow comes and she says she has too many things to do. Like what? Shop for shoes? Have lunch with Mrs. Lott? Irritating, I tell you.

I have lots to report, so get yourself some chicken treats and get comfy. For starters, Mr. Blair posted the cast list for *Peter Pan* today.

I could hardly wait. When the lunch bell finally rang, I flew down the stairs to the cafeteria to see who got what part.

But before I even reached the list, Andy Butterfield came running up to me in the hall and said, "Lorelei, you're playing Tiger Lily!"

"Oh. Who's Wendy?" I asked.

"Jenny Owens!" she said, racing back to the lunchroom.

I couldn't move.

Mud, how is this possible? It was supposed to be Saylor Creek. I mean, she sang better than anybody, and everybody knows it.

I leaned against the wall as the doors to the cafeteria were flung open and Drew Pembroke announced, "Saylor Creek's playing Captain Hook!" He and his buddies busted out laughing.

I got this sour taste in my mouth, and all I could think was *There must be some mistake.*

But there wasn't. I saw the list myself. Traced my finger from *Jenny Owens*, dot-dot-dot-dot, to *Wendy*. And *Saylor Creek*, dot-dot-dot-dot, to *Captain Hook*. I did it twice, just to make sure.

Of course, Jenny was at our regular lunch table being congratulated by what looked like the entire middle school. While on the opposite side of the cafeteria, Saylor was eating lunch all by herself. Jenny saw me and waved me over. "Come 'ere!" she said. But I pretended not to notice cause I didn't feel like going over there. I went to congratulate Saylor instead.

She was eating french fries. Dipping them in a lake of ketchup on her plate.

"Hi, Saylor," I said.

She ignored me.

"Congratulations on getting into the play."

"What do you care?" she mumbled.

"Well, I think you'll be really good as Captain Hook," I said.

She snorted.

"But I still think you should have gotten Wendy. I mean, I know Jenny's my best friend and all, but everybody knows you sang the best of anybody at auditions last week. We couldn't believe it. It was just amazing. Really amazing. So, anyway . . ."

Saylor stopped eating and looked up at me with her good eye. "Get lost," she growled.

So I did. Still, I was glad I went over and said what I said.

But wait till you hear this.

When I got home at four today, my dad was sitting on

the couch watching TV.

"Dad? What are you doing here?"

"I live here," he said.

Very funny. "I mean, why aren't you at work?"

And he said, "I took the afternoon off."

Remember the last time my father took the afternoon off? It was summer. He came home, and you, me, and Green Bean watched from my bedroom window as he cut down one of the pine trees in the front yard, then dragged it into the living room like a Christmas tree. He didn't even change out of his suit, or seem to care that it was ninety-eight degrees outside. He just threw his jacket and car keys on the grass, rolled up his sleeves, and started chopping.

By suppertime, the tree was covered with lights and ornaments and there was a huge pile of presents under it for everyone, even you and Green Bean. Remember that? It was exactly like Christmas in December. Except it was August.

My mom said it was a pale excuse for Dad to get satellite TV. She'd always been against getting it, and we soon found out why: sports. After that, Dad could watch them *all* the time—even on holidays. Even when the rest of us are being dragged off to church twice a year.

Still, my brothers and I thought Christmas in August was pure genius.

This afternoon, my dad and I had the whole house to ourselves. A miracle. I immediately plopped down on the sofa to watch baseball with him.

"How was your day, Peanut?" he asked.

"Well," I said, in my I-mean-business voice, "you're not going to believe this, but Jenny got the part of Wendy, and Saylor's playing Captain Hook."

My dad just looked at me. "Is that bad?"

Honestly, Mud, don't he and my mother talk? How many times in the last four days have I said that Saylor deserved to be Wendy?

I turned to my dad and explained the situation once more. Real slow like he was a flounder. I said, "Jenny wasn't as good as Saylor, plain and simple. None of the girls were. So how come Mr. Blair gave Wendy to Jenny? I'll tell you how come: cause Jenny's pretty and popular, and Saylor isn't."

"Oh, sweetie, I'm sure that's not why," Dad said.

"It is. It is why!"

"It can't be."

"Then what's the reason?" I demanded.

Suddenly my father wasn't so easy with the answers.

He sat back and stroked his chin cause it was a good question.

Finally he shrugged. "I don't know. I guess because people are people. But I do believe these things happen for a reason."

"You always say that," I grumped.

"Well, I believe it. And maybe it'll work out for Saylor next time."

Which is the whole point, Mud!

"There might not *be* a next time!" I blurted. "What if Saylor never tries out for the school play again?"

I could tell my father was getting frustrated with me, cause now he rubbed his forehead and heaved a huge sigh.

"Sweetie, Saylor's going to do what Saylor's going to do." Stupid grown-up gobbledygook. It made me mad.

A shaving commercial came on the TV, with a guy shaving and a beautiful blond woman coming up behind him and rubbing her face against his supersmooth cheek. It reminded me of Gretchen Terra and the *Us* magazine. *Now's my chance!* I thought. I ran to get it and showed my father.

"Look what I found in the attic."

Dad took the *Us* and stared at the picture of Gretchen on the cover. "Oh, sure, I remember this," he said.

"And look inside, look inside! There's a picture of you holding hands with her." I turned to the page with the corner folded down. "When was that taken?"

"That picture was taken in New York, about a month before your mother and I got married."

"But you and Gretchen are holding hands. I would never hold hands with a boy unless I really liked him," I said, confused.

Dad told me that he and Gretchen had quit dating about a year before the picture was taken. Then they both showed up at this fund-raising dinner, just by chance, and were suddenly surrounded by photographers. He was trying to lead her away from them when the photo was taken.

"It was nothing." He shrugged. "There were a lot more pictures of us *not* holding hands, but the magazine chose this one because they thought it would make a better story."

"Did you love her?"

"Nah, she was just a friend."

"Then you didn't want to marry her?"

"No. It never really came up. I always knew she wanted to try Hollywood, and I wanted to stay here and be a lawyer. We decided to go our separate ways. It was very friendly. After that I met your mom and *we* got married, had you and your brothers, and now we're living happily ever after."

"But Dad, you dated a movie star! That's incredible."

"She was just a girl, Peanut." He smiled.

"Oh no, not just any girl," my mother said.

Suddenly she was standing in the doorway. I nearly had a heart attack when I heard her voice, cause neither Dad nor I had seen her come in, and we had no idea how long she'd been standing there. It was kind of creepy. And it got me thinking, *Why does my mother always butt in when Dad and I are hanging out?*

My father cocked his head to the side. "What does that mean, Claire?"

"It means she was your first true love."

"Really? Wow, that's so exciting!" I grinned at my dad. "It must have been like going out with a queen. Did she live in a mansion with servants and a gigantic swimming pool?"

Mom looked really mad.

"Why are we even talking about this?" Dad sighed.

"Because your daughter wants to know why you were holding hands with somebody else a month before our wedding," Mom said.

My father rubbed his face. "And I told her, just like

I told you back then, I was trying to help Gretchen get away from the photographers. But that's not what this is really about, is it, Claire?"

"What do you mean?" She crossed her arms over her chest.

"We both know you were never that jealous of me dating Gretchen. You were jealous of her career."

My mother gasped. "That's a horrible thing to say, Theo!"

Dad's voice got louder. "Look me in the eye and tell me you didn't want to live in the spotlight like Gretchen."

"I n-never s-said that," Mom stammered. She bit her bottom lip and blotted her tears.

"Stop it! Stop! I just wanted to put the magazine in my time capsule," I shouted.

The sound of my voice startled everyone, even me. My mother actually looked at me like she'd forgotten I was there.

"What?" she whispered.

"Stop fighting! Just stop! I'm sorry I ever found the stupid magazine. I didn't mean to . . . I won't put it in my time capsule, okay, Mom? Just be nice to each other!" I was so angry my insides were shaking, and I felt like I was about to cry, so I ran up to my room, cause I didn't want to be like her, Mud. I didn't want to break down and make a scene like my mother.

My parents stomped around the house some more, and then I heard Dad leave. We had dinner without him.

This is all my fault, Mud. How could I wreck everything so completely? I didn't mean to, honest. I just thought it was exciting that Dad had dated a movie star.

Gunda and Jenny were right—I shouldn't have bragged about it. I should have just left the magazine where I found it, or thrown it away. Oh, Mud, what have I done?

Love,

Lorelei

Tuesday, October 25th

Dear Mud,

I'm in math class so I only have a second. But I had to write and tell you, my dad was asleep on the couch this morning, shoes and everything. Oh boy, I'm relieved.

More later.

Love,

Lorelei xo

Thursday, October 27th

Dear Mud,

Today will forever be known as Quitting Day.

This afternoon was the first cast meeting for the school play. Not really a rehearsal, more of a gathering, so Mr. Blair could hand out the scripts and the schedule and everyone could see, in person, who was playing what part. He also gave us a speech about how some parts may be bigger than others but that there are no stars in theater. He said the success of any play hinges on the strength of its ensemble.

Miss Dove, who will be Mr. Blair's assistant director, helped him hand out the scripts, cause Mr. Blair, being one-armed, couldn't hold them and hand them out at the same time. So she stood behind him and carried the pile. As Mr. Blair got to each student, he introduced us and announced what part we were playing. "Paul Windsor, congratulations. You're playing Peter Pan."

Paul beamed and put both hands over his heart like Miss America.

"Curley Portis, you're Nana, the dog. Lorelei Connelly, please honor us with Tiger Lily. Veronica Stavros, you're our lucky Tinker Bell."

"How is that lucky? Tinker Bell is just a light," whined Veronica.

"Not in our adaptation," said Mr. Blair, and moved on.

When he and Miss Dove got to Saylor, Mr. Blair made a big ta-da gesture with his one arm and said, "Saylor Creek, ladies and gentlemen, is our Captain Hook," and Miss Dove handed her a script.

But Saylor crossed her arms and refused to take it. "I don't want to," she said.

"You don't want to what?" asked Mr. Blair, arm akimbo.

"I don't want to play Captain Hook. I want to play Wendy."

There was a gasp, and all eyes locked on Saylor. I swear, Mud, you could have heard a whisker drop. Mr. Blair just stood there looking kind of sweaty and speechless.

Finally he said, "But Saylor, Jenny is playing Wendy."

"I know. It's not fair."

"How do you figure?"

"I'm a better singer than Jenny is."

There was an even bigger *Gasp!* I mean, Saylor's right, but I can't believe she had the guts to say it out loud. In front of everyone. Especially Jenny! Who, by the way, looked like she wanted to die. I actually felt bad for her. She tried to make a joke of it by rolling her eyes and making the "crazy" sign with her finger twirling around her ear. But you could tell her feelings were hurt, cause she was red from the neck up and kept her eyes on her shoes.

Mr. Blair said, "Saylor raises a good point, people. What you need to know is that there are many things that go into choosing a person for a particular role, and they're not always obvious to everyone. One of the first rules of acting is, the part doesn't make the actor, the actor makes the part."

Then he looked Saylor right in her good eye and said, "Meaning, if I asked you to be a tree in this production, you should be able to do that with as much commitment and enthusiasm as you would the part of Wendy. Or, in this case, Captain Hook."

Saylor laughed. "That's bunk."

Does she have double guts, or what?!

All of us, even Miss Dove, looked at Mr. Blair like *"Now what are you going to do?"* But he just stood there with this odd expression on his face: kind of tired, kind of amused, like he knew Saylor was right only couldn't let on cause then he'd be busted and no kid would ever listen to him again. So he pointed to the door and said, "Saylor Creek—"

She cut him off. "Save it. I quit!" she growled in that deep voice, and walked out.

End of first play meeting.

◎╱◎

Later:

It's after dinner now and I'm done with my homework, which is lucky cause there's plenty more to tell you about Quitting Day.

I got home from school just as Mom was getting home from lunch errands, and shoe shopping with some friends. We were both hanging our coats up in the closet when Dad called out from the kitchen.

"Are my girls home?"

Okay, Mud, as you know, this is the second time in three days my father has been home in the middle of the afternoon. It smelled like trouble to me, and I should have just gone straight up to my room. But Dad wanted to say hi, so I followed my mother into the kitchen where Dad was sitting at the table.

"What are you doing home in the middle of the afternoon again?" I said, going for a bag of peanut-butter-filled pretzels.

"I quit," he said, smiling.

I stopped. Mom cupped her ear and leaned forward as if she hadn't heard him right.

"I'm sorry, Theo, did you say you quit?"

"Yup."

"What did you quit?" Mom asked, eyebrows raised.

"My job."

"You quit your *job*?" she practically shouted.

"Yes, Claire, I quit my job."

My mother parked her hands on her hips.

"How long have you been thinking about this?"

"A while."

Mom put a finger to her temple. "A *while*?" She squinted as though the kitchen was suddenly too bright. "How could you not tell me before now?"

My dad shrugged. "Would you have tried to stop me?"

"Of course I would have!" she roared.

"That's exactly why I didn't tell you." Dad smiled.

My mother swayed and gripped the back of a chair for support. She was pale and tongue-tied.

"You really quit your job, Dad?" I asked.

"I really did."

The front door opened and slammed shut.

"I'm home!" called Teddy.

"In here," my mother hollered, without taking her eyes off my father.

Teddy appeared in the doorway still wearing his green down jacket.

"What are you guys doing?" he asked, heading for the refrigerator. Halfway there he stopped, turned, and noticed our father. *"Dad?* What are *you* doing here?"

"You all seem to have forgotten I live here." Dad laughed at his own joke.

Our mother was not amused. "Your father has quit his job," she spat, pronouncing each word in the sentence like it was a swear.

"No way," whispered Teddy.

Mom nodded.

"Can he do that?"

"Apparently, he feels he can," she said icily. Oh boy, she was mad. Maybe the maddest I've ever seen her. She stomped her foot and zeroed in on Dad. "The Connellys aren't quitters!" she bellowed.

But Dad never lost his cool. "Claire, I don't know what you're so worried about. We're going to be fine, moneywise. For heaven's sake, ever since I got the promotion at the firm, all you've done is complain that I'm not home enough. Well, now I'll be home, and you'll get to see me all the time."

Dad had a point. But Mom was in such a tizzy, he might as well have been talking to himself.

"But why did you quit, Theo? Why couldn't you have kept your job *and* figured out how to be home more?" she said.

"I'm burned out. I'm not happy. And you only live once, right?"

Teddy, meanwhile, was still rooted to the spot where he'd stopped on his way to the fridge, his mouth wide open, like the hinge was busted.

He erupted, "You can't quit!"

"I already did."

"But you're the dad!"

"Son, we're going to be fine."

"That's not the point. It's . . . not responsible."

Mom chimed in, "He's right, Theo."

Dad rubbed his forehead. "Gee, I thought you'd all be really excited about this." He sighed. "We are very, very, very lucky to be in this position. I quit because I wasn't happy. And if I'm not happy, I can't be the best dad and husband to my family. Not everyone can afford to make that choice, don't you see? So contrary to what you all assume, I *did* think this through. And I *do* have our best interests at heart." He walked over to Teddy. "I promise you, I *am* being responsible." He smiled.

But Teddy wanted none of it and bolted out of the kitchen.

"Lorelei, go upstairs, please. I need to talk to your father alone," my mother said.

I went to my room and shut the door. I lay down on top of the covers and stared at my poster of Jennifer Aniston and her beautiful smile. I could hear Teddy in his room, playing one of his end-of-the-world video games.

Green Bean came out of the closet and lay down next to my head. I don't know why Mom and Teddy were so upset, Mud. My dad made a good point. We hardly ever get to spend time with him anymore. And a happy Dad has to be a better Dad, right? Maybe he did the right thing, quitting.

I must have dozed off, cause I woke up with a jolt to the sound of the front door slamming. I got up and ran to my bedroom window just in time to see my father get into his car and drive away.

At dinnertime Ryan asked, "Where's Daddy?"

When Mom didn't answer, he started waving his fork in the air calling, "Daddy? Daddy?! Where are you?"

"He had to go out," our mother shouted over him crossly, and Ryan started to cry. Then, of course, she felt guilty. She pulled him into her lap.

Teddy and I looked at each other. Nobody spoke for

a long time. Oh boy, all that silence was giving me a stomachache. I had to make it better.

"Hey, guess what happened at school today. Mr. Blair was handing out the scripts for *Peter Pan*, and Saylor Creek said she didn't want to play Captain Hook, she wanted to play Wendy. And he said, too bad. So she said, I quit."

"Oh, my. What did Mr. Blair do?" Mom asked, sliding Ryan back to his own chair.

"He just watched her go! Can you believe that? I wanted to run after her, but I couldn't think of a good reason why she should stay and have to play a part she doesn't want to. Especially when she totally should have gotten Wendy."

"So who's going to play Captain Hook?" said Teddy.

"Maybe Mr. Blair will have to do it," I giggled.

"Well, that would be a first, a member of the faculty starring in the middle school play." My mother chuckled, which made Ryan giggle. And the next thing we knew, he was laughing so hard that milk was coming out of his nose. *Gross!*

"Ryan!" Mom scolded.

Which made him cry all over again. This time Gunda appeared from the kitchen and carried him upstairs.

When he was gone, Mom shook her head and apologized for ruining dinner. Then she took a deep breath and said she had something important to tell us. "Your father needs a break for a while," she said.

I wasn't sure what that meant, but the backs of my knees started to sweat.

"A break from what?" mumbled Teddy.

"Just a break. Your father needs some space. He's going to take a trip. See some things he's always wanted to see."

My mother was smiling when she said this, as though everybody's dad quits his job and goes on a road trip by himself. But her eyes were huge and sad.

"When's he leaving?" I asked.

"In a couple of days, I guess."

Teddy pulled his down coat around him tightly and stared at his plate.

I started to shiver on the inside and thought of my mom's aunt Fiona. Did I ever tell you about her, Mud? She went on a road trip too. Said she needed a break for a few days. So she kissed her family good-bye, promising she'd be back after the weekend. If they needed to reach her, she'd be at her mom's in Florida, she said. Only she never got there.

Of course everyone was worried sick. They thought she was dead in a ditch somewhere, and cops all over the state were told to keep an eye peeled for Aunt Fiona. Two months later, Uncle Fred got a postcard from Jamaica. All it said was "I quit. Love, Fiona."

Mom says Fiona's still there. Uncle Fred divorced her, and she married the mayor of some tiny town. They sell flip-flops and Aunt Fiona's famous macadamia brittle out of the back of their van.

After dinner, I overheard Gunda tell my mom that if she and my dad are through, she quits too.

Why would she say that, Mud? My parents aren't "through." Dad's just taking a break.

Needless to say, Gunda's announcement was pretty much the last straw for my mother, who went up to her room and locked the door.

I stayed in the kitchen and finished the dishes so Gunda could get Ryan ready for bed.

Upstairs, Teddy was back in his room playing video games. I poked my head in as I went by.

"What are you playing?"

"Final Fantasy."

"Are you winning?"

"Yeah. I think. . . . Oh! Yeah! No. Oh, crap! Well, I was until you came in," he griped, and swiveled around in his chair to face me.

"Sorry."

"It's okay. What do you want?"

Teddy's white rats, Sid and Nancy, woke up and scurried to their wheels. Why didn't you ever eat one of them, Mud?

I told Teddy what Gunda had said about leaving and asked him if he thought she knew something she wasn't telling us, like Mom and Dad are taking more than a break. Like maybe they're going to get a divorce. (I know, the *D* word. It felt worse than swearing.)

But Teddy just called me an idiot and accused me of turning everything into an international incident. "You heard Mom, it's no big deal. Dad just needs some space, is all."

"Space from what?"

"How should I know?"

"Space from us?" I worried out loud.

"I said I don't know. Now get out!" snapped Teddy.

"Okay, sorry," I said, and left, feeling pretty stupid.

I went down the hall to my own room, where I got ready for bed, which is where I am now.

I miss you so much, Mud. I look over at the bookcase where you used to sleep with Green Bean, and I feel like I can still see you there stretched out on your back, with your head upside down. But then I realize it's just a daydream, and I miss you even more. It's terrible and not fair.

Love,

Lorelei xoxo

☙

Later:

Ugh. I can't sleep. It's after midnight and my dad still isn't home. Where do you think he is?

I can't stop thinking about what Teddy said, either. About me fearing the worst and making everything into an international incident. That's not true, is it? I just worry. And Teddy's one to talk. He's wide-awake too. I can hear him playing video games down the hall, trying to save the world on his own.

Dear Mud,

Dad came home! I was still awake when he came into my room and kissed me on the head at 4:15 this morning.

"Where have you been?" I said, sitting up.

"Out."

He smelled of beer and wintergreen Lifesavers.

Suddenly, I just burst out crying. "You're not going to leave us, are you?"

My dad looked completely confused. "What? Where did you get that idea?"

"Gunda said if you and Mom are through, then she's leaving too. You can't go, Dad! You can't go!" I bawled.

Dad rocked me in his arms as Teddy appeared in the doorway.

"Sshhhhh, Peanut, everything is going to be A-OK." He looked up at my brother. "Your poor sister thinks the

77

world is coming to an end."

Teddy rolled his eyes. "She always does."

"Shut up, pinhead!" I said.

Dad shushed me. "No, no, none of that." He took my face in his hands. "Change is hard, Peanut. But I can tell you, your mom and I love each other as much as we always have. These last few days are just a nick in the pudding."

"A what?" said Teddy.

Now *I* rolled my eyes. "A nick in the pudding. You know, a stump in the road," I explained.

Jeez, sometimes my brother is dumber than a bag of dirt.

Teddy yawned and loped back to his room.

Dad stayed with me until I fell asleep. Boy, was I tired in school today. But it was worth it.

Love,

Lorelei

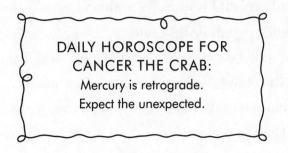

DAILY HOROSCOPE FOR
CANCER THE CRAB:
Mercury is retrograde.
Expect the unexpected.

Dear Mud,

Today is Halloween. Do they have Halloween in Heaven? They must. I picture all the ghosts coming down to Earth to see what's left of their moldy old carcasses in their worm-infested graves. Blech! How incredibly gross and fantastic at the same time.

Here on Earth, trick-or-treating was on Saturday, October 29th, instead of tonight—the real Halloween—thanks to the wimpy parents in our neighborhood association, who didn't want their kids out late on a school night. I mean, do you think the dead evil spirits, who look forward *all year long* to haunting on Halloween, knew that trick-or-treating was moved to the 29th, just so every kid could be in bed by eight tonight? Of course not! It was embarrassing, Mud. If I was an evil spirit, I'd be disgusted.

Anyway, I won't bore you with every

79

numbing detail of Saturday night, but Ryan dressed up as a bat this year. He was pretty cute. I went as a ghoul with a big bloody gash down my face. Jenny went as Scarlett O'Hara, and Veronica tagged along at the last minute as Madonna with a pointy bra. Typical.

By the end of the night, Jenny and I weren't speaking to each other. I'm telling you, if she doesn't get her own room at home, she's going to go crazy. And then she's going to drive *me* crazy! While we were trick-or-treating, she and Veronica kept whispering to each other and giggling, like whatever it was was the funniest thing in the universe. When I'd say, "What are you laughing at?" they'd just look at each other and say, "Nothing." Twits. After a while I got sick of them and left. So much for Halloween. It bugged me, though. I miss the old Jenny.

෴

For once my horoscope is right. It said I should be ready for anything, and guess what. Today we got a new nanny. His name is Lynn. Gunda's still with us, but when she said, four days ago, that if Dad goes, *she* goes, Mom got so mad, she told Dad she was going out to find a replacement.

"You wouldn't," said Dad.

"Watch me!" said Mom. The next day she came home with an armload of nanny references. She smacked them down on the kitchen table and said, "See?"

A day later she still hadn't read a single one of them.

"How come?" I asked her.

"Because I don't know where to start. And hiring a new nanny isn't actually the point. The point is, now your father and Gunda know that I mean what I say."

"But . . . not if you don't really go out and hire someone," I said. *(Duh.)*

Mom sat down at the kitchen table and put her head in her hands. "Oh dear. I know, I know," she whimpered.

Well, today when she played tennis with Sugar Harris, like she does most Mondays, Sugar came to the rescue. Cause by the time me, Teddy, and Ryan got home from school, Lynn was no longer Mrs. Harris's assistant— he was our new nanny.

Mom couldn't wait to introduce us to this short, beefy man with hair that looks like a cobweb of mouse-colored fur got caught on his head. "Lynn, these are my children: Teddy, Lorelei, and little Ryan. Children, this is Lynn. He's going to be teaming up with Gunda from now on to help around the house."

Yeah right, I thought. Gunda answered with a loud

crash! from the kitchen, letting us know that nobody's the boss of her and she wasn't going to show Lynn anything but the door.

Not that he cared. He was calm and cheerful as could be as he stuck his hand out for us to shake.

"How are you cats?" he said, with a big smile on his square face.

"Cats." He called us "cats," Mud! That made Ryan and me like him right away. We both shook his hand and said a friendly hello.

Teddy shook too, but only grunted.

That's about when our mother lost her mind. She put a hand on Lynn's cheek and said, "Sugar says you've had every job in the world." Then she leaned toward him like she had a secret. "She also says you have the whitest teeth she's ever seen. May we see them?"

Oh. My. God, Mud! What is wrong with her? Why does she want to embarrass us to death? I mean, she might as well wear her underwear on her head!

Dad was no better. When Mom called to him to come meet Lynn, he refused! So she leaned toward the new nanny again and said, "I'm awfully sorry. My husband is having a midlife crisis, and we never know, from one day to the next, which way the wind is going to blow. It sure keeps us on our toes, though." She laughed and wrapped her hands around her throat, pretending to choke herself.

Yikes! I started singing "The Star-Spangled Banner" in my head.

Oh, say, can you seeee . . .

Ryan threw himself on the floor and started bawling, and Teddy farted, nearly killing us all.

For you biographers, my brother is a master at waffling off the silent-but-deadlies. You don't even know what hit you. One minute you're minding your own business, sucking up the fresh air. The next, it's "Man down!"

Mom pretended not to notice we were all turning purple and breathing through our mouths so we wouldn't black out. But Ryan wouldn't let it go.

He stopped mid tantrum and howled with laughter. "Teddy cut one!"

And the rockets' red glare!

"Ryan, how rude!" My mother blushed and led the nanny away for a tour of the house. "I think you'll have a lot of fun here, Lynn. And if you have any questions, Gunda will be happy to help you," she lied.

The fact that Lynn didn't just turn around and walk out the door after all that made me like him even more.

Later I introduced him to Green Bean. We sat on the floor of my room, and he just waited for her to come over and sniff him. It took a while, but when she did, she flopped over on her side and purred nonstop.

"That's a miracle. She's usually really skittery around strangers," I said.

"Well, I spent a year in Nepal raising two orphaned snow leopards. Green Bean must sense I'm a cat person."

What can I say, Mud? It doesn't get any better than that.

Love,

Lorelei xoxo

Wednesday, November 2nd
11:09 A.M.

Dear Mud,

We're having a study hall instead of earth science class cause Mr. Flowers got food poisoning and had to leave all of a sudden.

It's lucky (I mean, not for Mr. Flowers) cause I really need to talk to you about something. I'll start at the beginning.

It turns out one of the jobs Lynn had, before working for Sugar Harris in the decorating business, was travel agent. A travel agent who specialized in beer-festival tours. Which means that even though Dad refused to meet Lynn two days ago, now they act like old friends, and one whole shelf in the fridge is filled with different beers from around the world.

Dad and Lynn have done several "tastings" of them already, which looks a lot like them just sitting on the couch, watching TV, and drinking. But Dad says I'm too young to understand what it's really about.

"Mom's old, and she doesn't understand it either," I corrected him.

He looked irked. "Yes, she does. She just thinks learning about beer is a waste of time," he replied.

So I admit I had begun to wish Dad would leave on his road trip already, cause as a couch potato, he's driving us all crazy. But this morning, when he was dressed, shaved, and ready to go before Teddy and I left for school, I instantly felt horrible for wishing him away.

"Are you leaving on your trip already?" I said, trying to be happy for him and stuff my own worry down at the same time.

"Heck, no. I'm off to the Golden Ale Brewery in Baltimore. I'm going to learn how to make my own beer." He grinned and patted me on the back.

I felt dumb, Mud. Dumb for feeling *bad* a minute ago, that he was leaving!

"I'm going to call my beer Connelly's Uncommon Brew. What do you think of that?"

"Fine," I said, not caring.

"Fine? It's great! I'm telling you, Peanut, this is the next big thing. So here's the deal. Lynn got me a private tour of this brewery, and I thought you'd like to come and see how it all works. You know, take a day off school and get a jump on the new family business."

"Dad, I'm eleven!"

"Well, I wasn't going to put you to work for a few years yet." My father chuckled to himself.

"No, thanks. I have a math test today."

But Dad was giddy with excitement. He took both my hands in his and started to waltz me around the room.

"You can take a math test any day. The brewery, on the other hand, will be like an advanced science class. Like visiting Frankenstein's laboratory. *Mmwu-ahh-ha-ha!*" He laughed like Dracula and twirled me around. It was a little bit funny, but mostly annoying.

I've only seen my father this excited about something one other time. It was right before Ryan was born, and Dad announced that he'd bought a sheep farm in Scotland and we were moving there in a month. Remember that, Mud? Teddy and I flat-out refused to go, and Mom was so angry she turned bright red and just sputtered like a motorboat. But Dad was completely delighted with him-self, skipping around the house like a kook, same as this morning.

Mom took us to visit Grandpa back then. She didn't even care that Teddy and I were going to miss school for a week. When we returned, everything was back to normal and the only rule was none of us were allowed to mention the sheep farm again.

Dad dipped me toward the floor.

"Okay, Dad, I have to go right now or I'll be late for school."

"And I'm telling you to play hooky." My father's eyes twinkled.

"No, I can't!" I said, and stood up to face him.

Dad bent down and put his hands on his knees so we were eye to eye. "As your father I'm giving you one-hundred-percent permission to play hooky for the day. We'll just tell your teachers you were on a field trip with me. You can write a paper about it afterward. Get some extra credit." And tapped the side of his head like he was thinking big now.

That was it, Mud. I was hopping mad. "I don't want to write an *extra* paper and get stupid *extra* credit, Dad! I can hardly keep up with the homework I have!"

Teddy wandered into the living room. "What's going on?" he yawned.

Dad put his arm around my brother and flashed his big lawyer smile. "Well, son, I'm talking your sister into spending the day with me at the Golden Ale Brewery, and I insist you come with us. What do you say? We'll be the Three Musketeers."

Teddy looked at me, confused. "What's he talking about?"

"He's talking about you and me cutting school and taking a tour of a beer factory with him, then writing an essay about it for extra credit. But I've told him a hundred times I have a math test today. On top of which I don't want to go to a brewery in Baltimore. I hate Baltimore. I just want to go to school like I do every Wednesday, cause I have a life too." I had to talk really fast before the words got knotted up with tears and stuck in my throat.

Teddy looked at Dad and said calmly, "Don't be a jerk. Not everybody wants to do what you want to do, Dad."

In a blink, the smile shrank from our father's face, and he grabbed Teddy with both hands and yanked him in close. Too close. It happened so fast, Mud. I couldn't believe it. Just a blur of bodies, noses almost touching. Teddy almost losing his balance, and Dad sucking up the tiny bit of air between them. "Don't you *ever* talk to me like that again. Do you hear me? *Ever!*" he said ferociously.

Teddy nodded, eyes huge and frightened. Afraid to breathe.

Then just as quickly, Dad let him go. He even straightened out my brother's jacket for him and handed him his book bag, as though nothing had happened.

"Well, all right, kids, have a good day. We'll do something together another time," he said casually.

And we left.

When we got to the corner, I was shaking. Teddy looked pale and upset too.

"Are you all right?" My voice quivered.

Teddy shrugged. He wouldn't look at me. "I don't want to talk about it," he said, and walked on ahead.

But *I* wanted to talk about it, Mud, cause it seemed like too much to keep inside. And Miss Dove says if you don't let your feelings out, your insides will turn to gunk and that's what gives you cancer and then you die!

That's why I had to write to you as soon as possible— to get it all out.

Ugh—I have a stomachache.

⟳

10:52 P.M.

The rest of the day was pretty crappy too. Jenny and I got into a huge fight just before English class cause I wouldn't lend her a pencil. I don't know why. I just didn't feel like it. So at lunch she refused to save me a seat. Then at play rehearsal, she told everyone I have a crush on Paul Windsor. Which is stupid, cause nobody has a crush on Paul Windsor. He's a wimp.

Meanwhile, Teddy got detention for stealing butter pats from the cafeteria and lobbing them onto the ceiling of the science lab. That is a whole new level of bad for my brother, the straight-A student, and obviously why he got caught. Cause everyone knows you can't just wake up to a life of crime. You have to get good at it.

When I got home from rehearsal, Dad was still away at the Baltimore brewery. It was weird to come in the front door and not hear some football game on TV or see him cemented to the sofa, just the big dent in the cushion where he usually sits.

By the time Teddy got home, Lynn and I were at the dining-room table figuring out my math homework.

"Hey, Teddy, how was detention?" Lynn asked cheerfully.

Oh, boy, did my brother give him the stinkeye. "Who told you?"

"The vice principal called and I answered," said Lynn.

"Well, detention is a joke," muttered Teddy.

Lynn nodded. "Yeah, I know a good deal about it myself. The thing is, dude, you're way smarter than I was at fourteen. And I'll bet you're smarter than most of your teachers, too. My point is, you don't need to throw butter at the ceiling to show them who's boss. You just have to mind your own business for a few more years; then you grab the world by the 'nads and make it groove." Lynn flashed a wide smile.

I swear, you could have knocked Teddy over with a whisper. It was like the nanny had told him, "Every night the world turns upside down and the ocean falls into the sky."

I guess Baltimore turned out to be pretty interesting, cause Dad missed dinner.

I hope while he was there he thought about what he did to Teddy. And I hope it ruined his day like it ruined ours.

In my next life I want to come back as a cat, Mud. That way, people will just pet me and play with me and I can sleep in the closet when I don't want people to bug me.

Love always and forever,

Lorelei ✕

Thursday, November 3rd

Dear Mud,

I'm not even writing down my horoscope today cause it said it would be an excellent day to write poetry. As you know, I hate poetry! So that's it—me and astrology are through. Kaput.

I'm here in the attic in my big comfy chair. It's cold and pouring rain outside, but I'm toasty under an old blanket I found. How's the weather in Heaven? Jenny says it never rains up there, but I told her she's a boob.

"Who's going to water the flowers?" I said.

Duh!

Dad got home from Baltimore late last night. Nobody waited up for him, but we all heard him come in on account of he slammed the door and yelled, "I'm home!" like it was the middle of the day.

Mom went to the top of the stairs and shouted, "Theo, keep your voice down!"

Too late.

Ryan woke up and started to cry. Which woke up Teddy, who yelled, "Shut your pie holes!" and threw a shoe against his door.

While Mom went to comfort Ryan, Dad plopped down on the couch and turned on the TV really loud. And Teddy threw another shoe at the door, then started playing doomsday video games.

The whole time, Green Bean and I lay perfectly still, with the covers pulled up to our noses, listening to rain slap against the window and the sound of my heart going *thwunk-THWUNK, thwunk-THWUNK*!

I don't know why I was scared, Mud. It just seems like things were pretty good not that long ago. Weren't they? But I already can't remember the last time my parents went a whole day without fighting. It makes me worry that something bad is going to happen.

At least Jenny and I are friends again. Miss Dove sent Jenny home early today cause she was snoring in English class. She died of embarrassment! But ever since Mrs. Owens put baby Jasmine in Jenny's room with her and June, Jenny hasn't gotten a wink of sleep.

Later, at *Peter Pan* rehearsal, Veronica volunteered to fill in for Jenny and play Wendy. But she doesn't know all Wendy's lines like I do. I actually know every line in the play. Which is why Mr. Blair chose me instead.

"Show-off!" sneered Veronica, and kicked me as I walked by.

So I socked her in the arm. I didn't even know I was going to, and I didn't care who saw me.

I used the trusty old knuckle punch that Teddy taught me. You ball your hand up into a fist and stick your middle knuckle out to make a sharp point, then *pow*!

As Teddy says, a little goes a long way, and Veronica let out a howl.

"Crybaby." I chuckled.

"That's it, Lorelei. You've forfeited your opportunity to play Wendy," declared Mr. Blair.

"But Veronica kicked me."

He held up his hand. "Don't want to hear it."

Veronica stuck her tongue out at me, then turned to the teacher all sugary. "Mr. Blair, can I do it?"

"No, I'm going to do it," he said.

Well, that shut both of us up. And even though Mr. Blair stank as Wendy, trust me, Mud, Veronica would have been way worse.

When I got home, Dad was gone again.

"On an errand," my mother said from deep within her walk-in closet. A moment later she emerged with an armload of high-heeled shoes. "Hey, how was rehearsal?" she asked.

"Jenny was sick, so Mr. Blair played Wendy today. What are you doing with all those shoes?"

"Lynn says I have the sexiest ankles he's ever seen. He thinks I should be a foot model. I can't believe Mr. Blair filled in for Wendy. Next time call me—*I'll* do it!" She beamed.

Nuh-uh! No way! Nohow! I shouted to myself. But out loud all I said was "I didn't know you wanted to be a foot model."

"Well, Lynn used to work at a modeling agency in New York. He said he'll make a few calls for me. Isn't that amazing?"

"Uh-huh. I thought he used to raise snow leopards in Nepal."

"The man has had many lives." Mom sighed admiringly and headed back into her closet.

"Right. Well, I have homework to do." I hurried downstairs.

Lynn was in the den playing go fish with Ryan, who was in a T-shirt and his underwear.

"How's it going?" I said.

"Fantastic. Ryan is becoming a totally awesome card shark," he said, and high-fived my little brother.

In four short days, Lynn has almost made Ryan into a human being. I sat on the floor and watched them play. "Mom says you used to work at a modeling agency in New York."

"Yup. Got any threes?" he asked Ryan.

"Go *fish*!" Ryan squealed.

"Do you think she could really be a foot model?" I asked Lynn.

"Totally."

"Okay, but don't tell her that if you don't really believe it. Cause she's been pretty crabby lately, and if the modeling thing doesn't work out, it'll only make things worse."

Lynn put his hand on my shoulder. "I fully get what you're saying. But before I worked for the modeling agency in New York, I worked for a shoe designer in Italy, and trust me when I tell you, your mother has perfect ankles." He winked and smiled.

Then the nanny let Ryan win, and my little brother clapped his hands gleefully. "I win! I win! I win!" he sang.

Maybe everything will be okay, after all.

Love,

Me

Dear Mud,

Oh my God! You won't believe what happened at rehearsal yesterday. I don't think this play is ever going to be anything other than a big steaming bowl of hair balls.

Paul Windsor, who's playing Peter Pan, is doing a great job, but he keeps getting beat up after school. Honestly, someone should tell him not to be such a sissy; then maybe the bully boys would leave him alone. But for now he has a black eye and his left arm is in a sling. How is Peter Pan going to teach the Darling children how to fly with a bum arm? Answer me that!

Then, Wendy is supposed to be English, but Jenny still sounds like she just stepped out of *Gone with the Wind*. If the line is: "John, there, just despises us," Jenny chews it up and spits out: "John, they-uh, just despi-i-ses us."

It's poke-you-in-the-eye awful, Mud. I can't figure out

why Mr. Blair won't say anything. But I shouldn't be surprised, I guess. For as long as I've known her, Jenny's had a knack for getting away with everything.

Curley Portis is playing Nana, the dog. (I told you, he's the sixth-grade class clown. His family just moved here from New Mexico.) Anyway, he keeps getting lost backstage and missing his entrances. Which makes you wonder: What's going to happen when he puts on the dog suit? Nothing good, I tell you. We'll probably never see him again.

Other annoyances: Since Saylor quit, Mr. Blair has decided *he* should play Captain Hook.

But I think the stress of acting *and* directing is getting to him, cause he's had laryngitis for a week. And he definitely has less hair than when we started. Plus, even if he was a good singer (which he isn't), you can't hear him, which is why he cut Captain Hook's song yesterday.

But the worst part is Mr. Blair doesn't know his lines. I mean, he sort of knows them, but when he's completely stumped, he starts doing this spastic pirate dance: hopping from one foot to the other, like he's trying to distract us from the fact that it's his line and he's not talking.

Well, today Mr. Blair and Paul were getting ready to rehearse the sword fight between Hook and Peter. Since

Paul takes fencing lessons, he was in charge of making up the fight. Even with his arm in a sling, Paul looked light and graceful, gliding around the stage like a figure skater. As it came time to start, he tossed Mr. Blair a sword without realizing that our director was already holding the Captain Hook hook and didn't have a free hand to catch it.

Everyone gasped and watched in horror as the sword twirled through the air and landed *splat-clatter-clatter* on the floor.

I don't know why it seemed so horrible, Mud, but after the sword hit the ground, the auditorium was dead quiet. You could have heard snow melt. Everyone just stared in shock from the sword to Mr. Blair, back to the sword, to Paul, who was turning all sorts of colors, like he was about to puke. Then he zipped offstage, yanking the sling off his bum arm as he went.

I'm telling you, Mud, it was like none of us had realized Mr. Blair was handicapped until that very moment. Which is good, I suppose. And yet, seeing him standing there looking helpless, the sword at his feet, made it seem as though we'd played a really mean trick on him. Except we never would! I guess no one thought about it—not even Mr. Blair—but you really need two hands to play Captain Hook. It made me think he probably forgets he's one-armed all the time.

Standing there, Mr. Blair started to look really shiny and hot, like someone had oiled his head. Then he moved quickly to Miss Dove and whispered something in her ear. She left and came back a few minutes later.

"Saylor's still here. She's in detention," reported Miss Dove.

"Go get her."

Which is how Saylor Creek walked into the auditorium to a round of cheers and applause from the entire cast *and* Mr. Blair. I'm willing to bet it's the first time she's ever felt like she belonged at our school.

Mr. Blair gathered us in a circle. "People, it's important to recognize your mistakes and own them. For this reason, Saylor, I'd like to say I made a mistake by allowing you to quit last week. We want you to come back and be our Captain Hook."

All of us stood there looking hopeful, cause we really wanted her to say yes—and not notice that she still wasn't being offered the part of Wendy. And, Mud, she agreed!

Right away I went up and said, "I'm really glad you're back, Saylor. The play's going to be a hundred times better with you in it."

She chewed on a piece of hair as she sized me up with

her good eye. Then she hauled off and slugged me in the arm. "Okay," she said, and waddled off.

It was great.

Love,

Lorelei

P.S. How do you like the bronze baby shoes I put on your grave today? They were my first pair of shoes. Mom had them bronzed when I grew out of them. She'll probably kill me when she sees them in the yard, but it serves her right for not taking me to the garden store like she promised she would weeks ago.

Dear Mud,

It's after dark, but I'm in the attic anyway, cause I've decided I need to be braver. Which means I'm going to try to do one thing every two weeks that scares me.

ⓒⓢ

In other news: I don't know if you'd say this is a good thing or a bad thing, but when Teddy and I came downstairs and saw Mom lying under the dining room table this afternoon, we didn't think that much of it. We did stop to look at her. Not cause we were worried, but cause she looked funny.

"Do you think she's okay?" I whispered.

"She's breathing," said Teddy, who didn't bother to keep his voice down.

She was lying on her back with one hand over her eyes like the see-no-evil monkey, and the other was stretched out to the side holding a piece of yellow paper.

We stared.

"She does look kind of peaceful," I whispered.

"Whatever," said Teddy, and took a pack of bubble gum from the pocket of his down jacket.

"What are you doing?" I gasped.

"Having a piece of gum. Do you mind?"

For all you biographers, gum—especially bubble gum—is one of my mother's pet peeves. She says it rots your teeth and makes you look like a cow chewing your cud. She never lets us have it.

"Where'd you get it?"

"I bought it, doofus. Do you want some or not?"

I eyed my brother suspiciously. It's not like him to just give stuff away; he usually wants something in return.

"A real piece? Not an ABC piece?" I said, not bothering to whisper anymore, either.

Teddy screwed up his face. "You're gross, Lorelei. Here." And he handed me the pack.

I love gum. Especially bubble gum.

We stood chewing, softening it up real good so we could blow some wicked bubbles. I pointed to the yellow piece of paper in my mother's hand.

"What do you think that is?"

"I don't know, dummy. Ask her if you care so much."

I shrugged quickly. "Who said I care?" But I kind of did.

I blew a gigantic bubble that stretched from my chin to my eyelashes, then expertly slurped it back into my mouth before it popped all over my face.

"Mom, are you okay?" I yelled, like she was deaf.

She sniffled and nodded, keeping her eyes closed. "Here, read this." She thrust the yellow paper at me.

My brother rolled his eyes and plunked down in a dining room chair. I sat cross-legged on the floor near Mom and read the letter to myself.

Dear Claire and Theo,

You guys are awesome! I totally enjoyed spending the last week with you and your great kids. I wish I could have stayed longer, but I got a call last night that my snow leopards are in danger, so I'm off to Nepal.

Claire, we'll do the foot modeling thing when I get back. Hang tight. You have awesome ankles. Lorelei, say good-bye to Green Bean for me. She's a special one. Theo, trust your taste buds, my man. I know you can make that excellent brew. Teddy, thanks for being exactly who you are. I respect that. And tell my buddy Ryan he's a chucklehead

He'll know what I mean. ☺

Okay, my friends, stay chilled.

Lynn

I couldn't believe it. Lynn. Gone. Just like that. And something told me he wasn't really coming back.

"Well, what does it say?" Teddy yawned.

"It's a good-bye letter from Lynn."

My brother didn't even flinch. He just pushed back from the table and said, "What's for dinner?" really loudly to show he didn't care.

But I don't believe him, Mud.

Gunda appeared in the doorway and said we were having roast chicken and potatoes. Ryan clung to the bottom of her gray skirt. His face was red and blotchy from crying, but Gunda looked pretty pleased with herself. She couldn't have been happier that Lynn was gone.

Dad came up behind her. "This is why we have Gunda, kids, because we can rely on her. She doesn't promise you things and then run off in the middle of the night."

"But why would he do that? We liked him so much. And he liked us." I didn't get it, Mud.

"Because he's an opportunist, a finagler, a phony," Dad said, staring at Mom.

Oh, brother. Suddenly the dining room felt way too crowded, even with one person under the table.

"I'm going upstairs," I said.

"Me too. Ry, come on," Teddy said, grabbing our little brother's hand. We ended up in Teddy's room. I sat on the bed and he knelt down in front of Ryan. "Hey, little man, how's it going? I'm sorry Lynn had to go," he said.

Ryan tipped forward and buried his face in Teddy's coat while Teddy stroked the back of his head. I never knew my older brother could be such a human being. Sid and Nancy, Teddy's white rats, came to the side of their glass cage and stood on their hind legs to see what was up.

When Ryan's crying-hiccups had mostly quit, Teddy wiped his face with his big down sleeve and said, "How about a game of Candy Land?"

"Really?" Ryan gurgled, eyeing Teddy hopefully.

"Really, dude."

"Yay! Let's play Candy Land!" Ryan giggled, jumping in place.

I wish I was like that, Mud, able to be sad one minute and overflowing with joy the next. Not caring that it might not last. Just wanting to hoover up every last drop while it did.

Teddy went to the hall closet where we keep all the board games and got Candy Land down from the top shelf. We played and played. Even when Teddy said he needed a break, he told Ryan and me we could stay in his room and keep playing if we wanted to.

I know! I didn't dare ask him why he was being so nice to us cause I didn't want him to change his mind. But Mud, if a stranger had walked by just then, I swear she'd never have known Teddy was my brother. She'd have thought, *Look at those good friends playing nicely together. Just average kids whiling away a rainy Sunday.*

Which is funny, cause Mom would die if she ever heard someone call us "average." She has a fear of blending in. "The worst thing you can be is *ordinary*," she tells us with panic in her eyes. But as soon as we're in a crowd, she doesn't want anyone to notice us, except to see how perfectly ordinary and blend-in-able we are.

Still, I've been thinking maybe ordinary *isn't* the worst thing you can be. I mean, look at Saylor Creek: She's definitely different and she doesn't have a friend in the world. I don't want to be like that. Or like my weirdo mother who takes naps under the dining room table. Or my oddball father who drinks beer and watches TV all day. Yikes! I'm just saying, maybe ordinary is perfectly pleasant. Like a movie you've already seen but don't mind if you can't remember.

Good grief, I'm actually looking forward to going to school tomorrow. Anything to get out of the house.

I found one of your catnip toys in the bottom drawer of my dresser today. Boy, did that make me miss you.

Love,

Lorelei xox

Tuesday, November 8th

Dear Mud,

I don't even know where to begin, but I'm writing from my bedroom cause Dad has taken over the attic. *MY ATTIC!*

That's right—I got home from *Peter Pan* rehearsal, I went up to the attic to start my homework, and Dad was there with a hot plate and two huge pots.

"Hi, Peanut. Isn't this great? Look at all this space up here," he said, like he was Christopher Columbus discovering the New World.

"I know; this is where I come to write and stuff," I said, taking a bunch of boxes off my armchair.

"Cool. I'll keep you company. I'm going to make my homemade beer up here." He beamed.

His stuff was already everywhere. A giant sack that said HOPS on the side, whatever that is, leaned against the table he had the hot plate on. Next to that were sacks of

110

"brewery sugar" and yeast. He stole my writing table to put books and spoons on. And around that were plastic tubs, a bottle capper, a hose, jugs of water, and boxes and boxes of empty brown bottles.

"Where'd you get all this stuff?" I asked, annoyed.

"Lynn ordered it before he left. I'm amazed. I didn't know he'd actually gone ahead and done it. Maybe I misjudged him." Dad smiled weakly.

Told you.

I sat in my chair and tried to do some homework, but my dad wouldn't shut up. He kept whistling "If I Had a Hammer." And when he wasn't whistling, he was reading his how-to-make-beer instructions out loud! Forget it.

He looked up from his pots and pans. "Hey, Peanut, where are you going?"

"I'm hitchhiking to California," I said, just to see if he was listening. Not.

"Great. See you at dinner." He smiled and went right on whistling.

Boy, I can't wait to be a grown-up so I can be a jerk whenever I want too, and nobody can say anything about it.

More later. If I ever write again, that is.

Love,

Me

P.S. I almost forgot. We have another new nanny. Her name is Happy. Yes, Happy. You'd think with a name like that, she'd be easygoing and chatty. But she was here most of the afternoon and only said about three words. Maybe she doesn't like kids. Which makes you wonder why she'd sign up for a job as a nanny. She's probably miserable cause she looks like a troll. There, I said it! She's kind of round and squatty with black curly hair and one long caterpillar eyebrow.

Oddly, Gunda has taken a shine to Happy. Or, at least, she said hello and showed her around the kitchen, which was more than she did for Lynn. Go figure.

Dear Mud,

I'm writing to you from behind some bushes, behind the gymnasium. Did you know there's a folding chair and a glass ashtray full of cigarette butts back here? I mean, can you see them from your cloud? Who do you think hangs out here?

So you want to know why I'm writing to you in the middle of the day?

Cause I'm cutting.

That's right, I, Lorelei Lee Connelly, am playing hooky for the first time in my life.

Jenny says I'll be grounded forever when my parents find out that I cut. And she's probably right, but who cares? I've never been grounded before. It might be delightful.

⊘⊘

113

Nine minutes later:

Oh my God, I had to quit writing cause you'll never guess who was just here: Matt Newsome, the school bully! He came around the corner of the building and was so startled to see me sitting here, he actually yelped. I told you, Matt's huge. And stinky. And just as ugly as ever.

When he got his cool back, he leaned over me, blocking the sky from my view. "Hey, loser, what are you doing in my chair?" But before I could answer, he remembered who I was. "Wait a minute, you're Teddy Connelly's little sister." Then his eyes got wide and fierce. "Are you following me? I oughta punch your loser lights out!"

My throat was mitten dry—even air got stuck going down. But I stayed put in that chair. I poked my chin out and said, "No, I'm not following you, and you won't punch me cause if you were going to, you would have already."

Matt bent down and put his hands on his knees. He smelled like toast and sour onions. P.U.

"You think you know me? You think you know what I'm going to do?"

"No," I peeped. I was suddenly trembling beneath my coat. And not cause it was cold!

"Good," he snorted, and stood up straight.

I waited.

"You have some guts for a pip-squeak."

"Thank you."

"Now get out of my chair!"

"Stop yelling—it's rude!" I yelled back.

And he laughed. Not exactly a friendly laugh. More of an I-want-to-kill-you laugh. But it seemed like a good sign, just the same, until he lifted me out of the chair by both my arms and stood me on my tippytoes so we were almost eye to eye and he could glare at me better.

"Listen, nerdlinger, if you don't stay out of my chair, I'll tell the principal you were back here smoking weed, and you'll get suspended. Then your mommy will be *weally, weally* mad at you," he snarled.

I wriggled free, and I'm sure he expected me to start blubbering like a baby cause I *was* pretty scared. But I didn't, Mud. I stayed right where I was and laid it out for him.

"First of all, Principal Sanchez would never believe you if you told him that. He'd say, 'Lorelei? You must be mistaken. She never does anything bad.'

"And second, then he'd know you were back here too. And *you'd* get suspended *with* me, which is probably no big whoop for you. But what if the whole school found out we were suspended together? They'd want to know why you were hanging out with a measly sixth grader. They might even think you *like* me. And that would be the end of your reputation as the meanest kid in school. So go ahead, rat me out. See if I care."

Well, that shut him up. Matt looked at the ground and wiped his nose on his pasty bare arm. Then he kicked the chair over. *Ka-BLAM!* I jumped and he chuckled to himself. He pulled a cigarette out of his pocket and leaned against the brick wall of the gym.

"Smoke?" he said, offering me the pack.

"No, thanks."

He shrugged and lit a match on the bottom of his shoe. His shoe, Mud! You should have seen it. The wind kicked up and he shivered.

"Where's your coat?"

Matt dug his heel into the dirt. "I must have left it in my locker." He smirked.

But come to think of it, I've never seen Matt wear a coat, ever.

He puffed on his cigarette and stared up at the gray and white sky. I leaned my back against the gym wall and snuck a peek at him. There were goose bumps up and down his arms. Halfway through his cigarette he started to shuffle off.

"Where are you going?"

He turned and lunged at me. "What did you say?"

"I just asked you where you were going." I gulped.

"None of your loser business!" he yelled right in my face.

"Okay!" I yelled back. But I swear, I nearly hopped out of my skin, he's so scary. Then he grabbed me by one arm.

"Let's get this straight." He scowled. "If you tell anyone I left campus, or that you even saw me today, I will hunt you down and gut you like a dog. Then I'll spread your guts on your front porch so the cockroaches can choke on you."

I nodded, and he took off across the football field.

Oh my God, Mud, I've never been so frightened in my life. It was fantastic!

☙☙

8:36 P.M.

Dear Mud,

Jenny was right—I got in big trouble for cutting math class today. My math teacher (aka: The Water Buffalo) called Mom tonight to say she hadn't seen me in class today, and I wasn't on the absentee list, so she wanted to make sure I was okay.

Of course, my mother told her I was fine and she

couldn't imagine why I had missed math, and promised to get to the bottom of it. She hung up the phone and turned to me. "That was Ms. Kurtz."

"Oh, really? What did she want?" I smiled innocently as though I was expecting good news.

"She says you missed her class today. Is that true?"

"Um . . . yes. I decided I was better off not going to math today."

My mother crossed her arms. "Excuse me? Lorelei, are you telling me you *cut* math class?"

She said "cut" like it was a swear.

"Yes, but I had a good reason."

"It better be a *really* good one," she warned.

Honestly, Mud, I don't know how I come up with this stuff sometimes. Cause there'll be nothing in my brain but gobbledygook, then all of a sudden, *pow!* A thought hits me and it's so brilliant I scare myself.

"Mother," I said, "I'm eleven years old and I never do anything I'm not supposed to, which means I'm so boring I might as well be dead. I knew if I didn't start doing some exciting stuff right now, this second, I'd end up like Dad. I'd quit my job, live on the couch, and drive my family completely crazy. Therefore, cutting math class now is like an insurance policy against being a crummy grown-up."

I could tell by the long pause that my mother knew it was a darn good argument. She probably even wished she'd thought of it herself. So I was totally surprised when she said, "You're grounded. One week."

"What? But Mom, you know I'm right!"

"No, I don't. Grounded. Two weeks."

"Mom!"

Is everyone crazy, Mud? I could feel my insides boiling as I stomped toward the stairs. "You're not the boss of me," I called over my shoulder.

"Lorelei Lee Connelly, don't you dare walk away from me like that! I'm not done with you," my mother shouted. I stopped.

"What?" I said under my breath.

Dad came in the front door.

"Theo, where have you been?" Mom demanded.

"I had some stuff to do," he said easily.

"You've been gone all day!"

"Just last week you were complaining I never get off the couch. Make up your mind."

"Don't change the subject!" she roared.

"Claire, what is the matter with you?"

Mom planted her feet and put her hands on her hips. "Your daughter cut school today, Theo."

"I didn't cut school. I cut *math* class," I corrected her.

"Don't interrupt!"

"Fine," I mumbled, and started toward the stairs again.

"Where do you think you're going, young lady?"

"You said I'm grounded, so I'm going to my room!" When I got there, I locked the door.

I could still hear Mom and Dad arguing about where he'd been. A few minutes later Mom was outside my door.

"Lorelei, hear me loud and clear. I will not tolerate this behavior. You are grounded for the rest of your life!" she thundered.

"Fine! Cause you know what? That's impossible," I informed her.

"All right, young lady, no dinner for you."

"Good!" I shouted, and she left.

Gee whiz, what a day, Mud. Do you think if I'm grounded for the rest of my life, I still have to go to school? I hope not. I'd still like to be in the play, but maybe I could skip everything else. Then I could get a job and get my own apartment.

Think of it: me and Green Bean out on our own. That would be tickety-boo! (Grandpa used to say that all the time. It means "awesome.")

I guess I better do some homework on the off chance it doesn't work out that way.

Love,

Lorelei xo

⊘⊘

9:22

Mom just found the bronze baby shoes I was using as your tombstone. Boy, is she mad. Mad on top of being mad! Big deal. I'm already grounded for life. What else can she do to me? The bad news is there's no telling when Mom will take me to the garden store now. But I'll find a way, Mud. I'll find a way.

Dear Mud,

It turns out even if you're grounded for life, you still have to go to school. The perk is, I've sort of become a celebrity for cutting class yesterday. Even Veronica said I could jump in front of her in the lunch line. I only said yes so I could stand right behind Bo Emerson. He smells warm and sunny, like the beach.

When he saw me, he said, "Hey, Lorelei."

"Hi," I said.

Veronica butted in. "Hi-i-i, Bo."

"What's going on, Veronica?" He smiled, not really looking at her.

"Nothing," she giggled, and popped her chest out. Who is she, Jessica Rabbit? Blech. She's so obvious it's nauseating. Plus, her teeth are too small for her gums. There, I said it.

The line moved ahead. "What are you getting?" Bo asked me.

"Probably fish sticks and mashed potatoes."

"Me too," he said. And then he asked me where I was sitting.

I almost fainted.

Before I could say anything, Veronica stuck her head in between us. "I saved Lorelei a seat over by me."

"Really?" I said, cause Veronica has never saved me a seat in her life. Not even when Jenny's at school, and she was absent today.

"Of course I saved you a seat, dummy. Bo, there's a seat for you, too," she said, and headed for her table.

"Um . . . " Bo hesitated, looking at me like he'd rather go on a hunger strike than sit next to Veronica. "No, that's okay. I'm going to sit with Colin and Jeffrey today. Thanks. See you later, Lorelei."

"'Bye."

I could have killed Veronica. Not only cause she drove Bo away, but when I got to where she was sitting, she hadn't saved me a seat at all! Figures.

I have math after lunch on Thursdays. And today The Water Buffalo made me sit up front.

"So I can keep an eye on you," she said, sticking her finger in my face.

Sometimes grown-ups are beyond thick. I mean, if I was going to cut class again, I wouldn't go and then leave in the middle of it. I wouldn't show up in the first place!

At the end of math, The Water Buffalo handed me a pink slip and said, "You have detention after school."

"I can't go today. I have play rehearsal this afternoon," I explained sweetly.

Ms. Kurtz raised her penciled eyebrows and said in her hootiest, snootiest voice, "You should have thought of that before you decided to skip my class yesterday, Miss Connelly."

I don't care if she is my teacher, Mud, I wanted to sock her.

I found Mr. Blair in the hallway, but before I could tell him I wouldn't be at rehearsal, he said, "Lorelei, I know you have detention this afternoon, so you're excused from rehearsal. But if you miss one more, I'll have to replace you."

"What if I get sick?"

"Don't," he answered, and glided away.

◎◎

For all you biographers who never broke a rule in your life and wish you had, I'm here to tell you, you totally should have. Cause detention is a joke! You can hardly even call it a punishment. It's just a study hall, where nobody cares if you study. Plus, you get to see all the bad kids who aren't in your grade. It's fantastic. Well, I wasn't that crazy about this bunch of ninth-grade boys chucking paper balls at my head. But—get this—Matt Newsome came to my rescue!

He was ten minutes late, but Mr. Melon, the detention monitor, hardly seemed to notice. I guess Matt's been there so many times, he comes and goes as he likes and everybody lets him.

When he walked in, I was sitting up front. And as he passed me he gave me The Nod. The Nod, Mud! Then he slid into a desk next to the bratty ninth-grade boys and said, "No, dudes, not her."

Can you believe that? Matt Newsome said "not her"! And the boys started throwing paper balls at Lars Lund instead. He's an eighth grader in Matt and Teddy's class.

I'm sure you're wondering why we were all in detention together, middle schoolers mixed in with upper schoolers.

Well, Mrs. Romberg usually monitors upper school detention, but her liver exploded, or something, so she's in the hospital watching soap operas and eating Jell-O. At least that's what I heard two teachers say when I got to

Mr. Melon's "coop." (That's what they call the classroom where detention is: the coop.) So the school's been lumping all the students together until they find Mrs. Romberg's replacement.

Anyway, like I said, I thought detention was fantastic. Like a zoo, with all the kids you hear about but never get to see up close. Felicity Jackson, for example. She's an eighth grader. Teddy says she knows how to hot-wire a car.

And Jorge Peña, who's in my class, was asleep in the corner. I took a long hard look at him for the first time. He doesn't look like a kid who sets things on fire. But you can't judge a moose by his sweater.

And then there's Matt Newsome and his buddies, of course, who didn't even pretend to do any work. They just goofed off and played cards the whole time.

When I got home, I told Mom I'd finished all my homework already. As a reward, she said I could watch half an hour of TV before dinner.

I grabbed Green Bean and we climbed into my parents' bed. Just as I was settling in, Happy knocked on the door. "Can Bob watch TV with you?" she asked.

"Who's Bob?"

"Me!" yelped Ryan, and took a flying leap onto the bed.

"Your name's Ryan," I said, making room for him beside me.

"No, *Bob*!" squealed my little brother.

"It's easier to remember than 'Ryan,'" grunted Happy, and ducked out of the doorway before I could ask her what flavor of moron she is.

Green Bean got under the covers, and Ryan and I pulled the pink satin comforter right up to our chins and watched half an hour of *The Wizard of Oz*.

I'll say it again: Saylor Creek sings just like Judy Garland. And I sure wish I had a pair of ruby slippers like Dorothy, cause I'd wear them to school every day and click my heels together for wishes all the time.

Love,

Lorelei xoxo

P.S. Your new grave marker is the blue and red ashtray I made in second-grade art. Remember that thing? Mom keeps it on her desk filled with paper clips. So I dumped out the paper clips, and ta-da! New tombstone-for-now.

Dear Mud,

I have something to tell you but I don't know where to start. This thing happened today, after school, and it's giving me the heebie-jeebies.

Jenny and Veronica and I were walking home after play rehearsal, which was cut short cause Paul Windsor is getting a cold. I know, disaster! Anyway, we decided to stop at the drugstore for some candy. Even though I'm grounded and I'm supposed to go right home, I didn't care.

Inside the store, Veronica peeled off looking for boys she might know, while Jenny and I went to look at the makeup. We tried on lipstick and rouge and nail polish, and when we got bored with that, we bought some Rolos and Junior Mints and sat outside on the bench in front of the store to wait for Veronica.

"Hey, Lorelei, isn't that your dad?" Jenny said,

pointing across the street.

I looked up, and sure enough, it was him. I was about to call out, cause he hadn't seen us, but he was with this redheaded woman I didn't recognize.

"Who's he with?" asked Jenny, as I wondered the exact same thing.

"I don't know."

I stood up to get a better look. And I couldn't believe what I saw, Mud. They were holding hands!

"Come on; hide," I whispered to Jenny, and yanked her around the corner of the building, out of sight.

I made her stand behind me so she couldn't see my father and the woman. But I never took my eyes off them. My heart slammed against my ribs as I watched them laugh and stroll down the block, chummy as can be. They stopped in front of a parked car. It was Dad's car, and he leaned against the front of it. Then my heart stopped. She kissed him, Mud. And he kissed her back—on the lips! In front of the whole world!

I slid down the wall of the drugstore, next to Jenny. My insides felt hot and soupy.

"Are you okay? Are you sure you don't know that lady?" she asked.

All I could do was shake my head no, cause I couldn't get any words out.

"Maybe she's a new friend of your parents', and you just haven't met her yet," Jenny suggested hopefully.

I shrugged. Still no words.

My stomach felt really icky now. I picked up my backpack and told Jenny she could wait for Veronica by herself—I had to go.

"Okay, call me later," she said, and gave me a tight squeeze.

I took the long way home and kept closing my eyes as I walked, but I couldn't erase the picture of my dad kissing that woman from my head. Who is she? Why were they together? I mean, strangers probably thought she was my dad's girlfriend. But they shouldn't think that, Mud. They should be thinking, *That's Lorelei's father. He's married with kids and a cat.*

Then it hit me. *Oh no!* Those days and nights when Dad goes out and we ask him where he's been, and he just says, "Out." Maybe he's with her.

I stopped in the middle of the sidewalk and thought about that. Thought about my dad having a secret life we don't know about. It made me dizzy. And it made me afraid that anything could happen, and me and Teddy and Ryan will always be the last to know—when it's already too late.

I ran the rest of the way home, burst through the front

door, and went straight up to the attic to be by myself and think. Just my luck. Dad was already there. He'd beaten me home and was standing over his hot plate and pots again.

"Hi, honey," he said, stirring something that made the whole room smell like sweaty armpits. P.U. I had to breathe through my mouth.

I marched right over and stood in front of him. The words were crashing around inside me, and I was ready to let him have it.

Don't "Hi, honey" me, I was ready to say. *Who is that woman you were with this afternoon? Where'd you meet her? Does Mom know her? Does she know you two were holding hands and kissing?*

But nothing came out. Nothing but deep trembling breaths as the courage drained right out my toes. I felt so stupid, Mud!

In real life, the conversation went like this:

Me: "Hi."

Dad: "Are you okay, Peanut? You look a little out of breath."

Me: (shrug.)

Dad: "What did you do today?"

Me: "School."

Long pause.

Me again: "What did *you* do?"

Dad: "I moved on to 'phase two' of concocting Connelly's Uncommon Brew. Every day it gets closer to being beer. Isn't that exciting?"

Me: "Sure." A lie.

Another pause.

"What else did you do today?" I asked.

"Not much." Dad smiled.

"Really?"

He stopped stirring the pot and eyeballed me suspiciously. Even a little mean. Finally he said slowly, "I saw some friends."

"Anybody I know?"

"Sure. Dale and Mercedes Quinton. They have the twin boys who are Ryan's age, remember?"

"Yeah, I remember. I hate those twins. They're spoiled and they always pull my hair," I told him.

Dad laughed and started stirring again. His manner was easy now.

The thing is, Mud, Mercedes Quinton has black hair, not red. So who else was my dad with this afternoon?

He looked at his watch.

"Don't you have homework to do, Peanut?"

"Yup, I sure do."

But before I left, I stared at him good and hard. Kept staring until he looked away first. That way he'd know that I know he's up to something. Not that it made me feel any better, or any less confused.

I got back to my room, but I couldn't sit still. I had to go for a walk. So much for being grounded for life. Nobody even tried to stop me, or remind me I had forgotten my coat, though I hardly noticed the cold. I'm telling you, anger like that makes you hot, hot, hot!

I walked and walked around the whole neighborhood. Don't even know where I went, exactly. I just had to keep moving. At 6:30 I went home for dinner.

I thought Mom was going to yell and ask me where I'd been, but nobody said boo about my being gone.

Dinner was fried chicken from the diner up the street, cause even though Gunda doesn't mind Happy, she's still mad at Mom for hiring extra help, so she's been refusing to cook just to get back at her.

All Mom wanted to talk about was my rehearsal.

"How'd it go?" she asked.

"Fine."

"I'd love to come watch one afternoon."

"You're not allowed," I said.

"Why not?"

"Cause Mr. Blair says no one's allowed until we're ready." He didn't really. I just wanted her to quit asking me dumb questions.

Now I'm in bed with Green Bean, who's finished with her bath and snug underneath the covers. I swear, she sleeps like a stone. If she weren't snoring, you'd think she was dead. I wish I could sleep like that. I'd just close my eyes and keep them closed until spring. I figure by then everything will have to be fine and I won't feel this sad and full of holes.

I miss you, Mud. Sleep tight.

Love,

Lorelei xx

Dear Mud,

Mr. Blair called a special rehearsal today cause he said we need it. I love being at school on the weekends. I know that sounds weird. But running through the halls with nobody to stop you, peeking into the upper school classrooms (which you could never get away with on a school day) is like being an international spy.

Mr. Blair has decided that from now on, we will start rehearsal with a theater game, or exercise. He says it will sharpen our concentration and build trust among the cast members. He's big on that. He tells us at least four times a week, "You must have trust onstage, people. That is the foundation of a successful ensemble."

Today we played "blob."

Mr. Blair explained: "It's similar to tag. You're going to spread out and stay *within* the boundaries I've set down here." He pointed to four bright pink plastic cones that made the corners of a square. "I will choose one person to be the blob leader. Then the rest of you will do your best to avoid being tagged by that person. When you are tagged, you immediately become part of the blob, forcing you to work together. See how that works?" He wiggled his eyebrows meaningfully. "We'll keep going until everyone is blob-incorporated."

Mr. Blair chose Lucia, who's playing Michael (Wendy's youngest brother), to be the first tagger. But as soon as everyone started to run away from her, she plopped down in the middle of the square and began to cry. So we had to start over with Curley as the tagger.

Curley may not be the smartest clam in the mud, but he's fast!

Of course, he went after Veronica first cause he has a giant crush on her. Wouldn't even look at anybody else until he got her. Jenny and I thought it was funny. But Veronica was mad as a wet hen. After that they ran around and got Jenny, Drew, me, and Paul. Until everyone was tagged except Saylor.

I know she's used to that, Mud, but I still felt bad for her. And, of course, no matter how slowly she ran, the blob ran slower. So I ran over and tagged her myself. Man, we were a stinky blob. I'm telling you, boys and Saylor are stinky.

Mr. Blair said the point of the exercise was to make rehearsal go more smoothly. Didn't.

Drew, who's playing Smee, sang off-key in the pirate songs, which he never does. Veronica/Tinker Bell, who's taller than Paul/Peter Pan, knocked him down *three* times today, instead of the usual two. (She pretends it's an accident, but everyone knows it's not.) And Curley pulled the head off the teddy bear Lucia needs to play Michael, cause she called him a fatty.

So I'd say rehearsal was just barely above awful.

Still, it was the only time today that I forgot about seeing my dad with that redhead.

I wish I'd never gone to the drugstore yesterday. I wish I'd gone straight home like I was supposed to. Then I wouldn't have to keep this gigantic secret to myself.

Love,

Lorelei

Dear Mud,

Three hours ago I locked myself in my room and refused to go down for dinner even when Mom begged me. Now I'm starving and I wish I had a peanut butter and jelly sandwich. Maybe when everyone has gone to bed, I'll sneak downstairs and make myself one. At least I know I won't run into Dad down there, cause he left with a suitcase an hour ago. I watched him go from my window.

Anyway, I'll back up and start from the beginning.

The day was going pretty well. To everyone's surprise, Teddy had volunteered to design the labels for Dad's homemade beer. I don't know if you've noticed, but Teddy's been ignoring Dad as much as possible since Dad grabbed him that day we didn't want to go to the brewery. So for Teddy to say he'd make labels was a super nice thing for him to do.

I spent the afternoon at the dining room table doing a jigsaw puzzle of the solar system with Happy. Well, Happy wasn't doing anything, actually, except breathing through her mouth and watching. The house was peaceful for three whole hours today.

Then the phone rang.

I answered. It was Eileen Lott, one of my mom's good friends. She sounded upset and didn't even say hello. Just started with, "Oh, Lorelei. Oh, dear. Um . . . I need to speak to your mother."

"Okay. Hang on a second, *pleeeeze*." I covered the phone with my hand and yelled, "Mom! It's Mrs. Lott for you!"

"All right, you don't need to yell," she said.

My mother picked up in the downstairs hallway by the stairs, and I went back to my puzzle.

From where I was sitting, I could see her take a seat in the fancy chair Grandma made that needlepoint cushion for. (The one you liked to sharpen your claws on, remember?) Mom's head was cocked to the right and she seemed to just be listening to Eileen blather on. Then she leaned forward with her elbows on her knees. A deep wrinkle spread across her forehead, and all of a sudden she sat bolt upright, her mouth wide open in shock. "I have to go," she said in a hoarse voice, and hung up quickly.

She sat, frozen in the chair, staring at the wall, like somebody had emptied out her insides. I've never seen her look lost like that, Mud. As though she didn't know who, or where, she was.

It gave me the meemies.

Before I could ask my mother what was wrong, she headed for the living room, where Dad and Teddy and Ryan were watching football on TV. She told my brothers to go upstairs. But when they saw me and Happy in the dining room, they came and sat with us at the table instead. We all knew something big was about to happen. Even Ryan didn't say a word.

We heard Dad say to Mom, "Claire, move. I can't see the game."

She switched off the TV.

"That was Eileen Lott on the phone. She told me she saw you on Wisconsin Avenue on Friday, holding hands with a redheaded woman. *Holding hands and kissing.*" Pause. "Is that true, Theo?"

Teddy and I each had a puzzle piece in our hands ready to go, but we were frozen in midair. My heart was beating so loudly in my ears, I was sure my brothers and

Happy could hear it.

"Is it true, Theo?" Mom repeated.

It's odd, Mud—we couldn't really hear Dad's answer. All we heard was the soft *s* sound of his "yes." But it was all the answer we needed.

Have you ever heard the expression *the calm before the storm*? It means the air gets really still before a huge hurricane or something comes and destroys everything. Well, that's what it was like. Dead quiet, and then *BLAMMO!* The storm hit.

Mom and Dad started shouting. Ryan sobbed quietly into his tiny hands. And I got a stomachache.

"That's it," Teddy said. He threw down the puzzle piece he'd been holding and marched into the living room. Happy pulled her chair up next to Ryan and put her arm around him, Gunda watched from the kitchen, and I followed Teddy.

Dad was pacing, wringing his hands, not looking at Mom, not answering as she demanded he tell her what was going on. When she saw us come into the room, she turned quickly. Her face was red and sweaty, and a clump of dirty-blond hair had come untucked from her ponytail. "Your father is leaving for a while. I've asked him to leave," she huffed.

After that, I started pinching the back of my hand cause I couldn't feel anything, Mud. Just numb.

Teddy went up to her. "Why don't you let Dad talk first? You never let people talk!" he bellowed.

Well, that shut everyone up. Except Happy. From the dining room we heard, "Come on, Bob, let's go play in your room."

I peeked around the corner and saw her and Ryan head for the stairs.

In the living room Teddy turned to Dad. "Who's the redhead?"

I was sure Dad was going to have a good answer right on the tip of his tongue and it would make everything all right. But he paused, Mud, and stared out the window like he hoped to find the answer at the foot of the big elm tree. My heart sank.

Teddy stomped out the front door and slammed it so hard the living room windows rattled. Gunda disappeared into the kitchen. Hot tears rolled down my cheeks as Mom came up behind me and quietly told me to go to my room. But I exploded.

"No!" I faced my dad. "*I* saw you with that lady too! I hid behind the drugstore with Jenny cause I didn't want *her* to see you. I didn't want *anyone* to see you!"

I stood there shaking all over, crying, my stomach

hurting, waiting to see what my parents would do, what they had to say for themselves. And the answer is a big fat nothing! They just gawked at me. I couldn't believe it! I ran up to my room and locked the door. And that's how come, three hours later, I'm still here, starving, headachy, and afraid, wondering what I'm supposed to do now.

God, if you're listening, I'd like it if absolutely nothing happens tomorrow. Please make the day as boring as possible. I won't mind at all.

Oh, Mud, some days the sadness and missing you are so huge, it feels like they'll never go away. And the only thing that makes me feel better is knowing that you're listening. Thanks for always being there.

Love,

Me xo

Dear Mud,

I've been thinking. I need something to take my mind off my dad being gone, cause otherwise I'll just be sad all the time. I remember Grandpa used to say he tried to learn something new every day of his life. Even if it was just a small thing. I like that. And I've decided if I'm going to be a writer I should learn a new word each day.

Here's how I'll pick it. I'll close my eyes, let the dictionary fall open to any old page it wants, and point, eyes still closed. Wherever my finger lands, that will be my Word of the Day.

Today's selection is **odiferous** (adj.): *having or giving off an odor.*

"Teddy is sweaty and *odiferous* after soccer practice."

Well, Gunda left this afternoon. She was crying. And even though she has always sided with my dad and said she would go as soon as he did, it didn't seem like she really wanted to.

She said good-bye to each of us kids separately, so I don't know what she said to Ryan and Teddy, but to me she said, "Lulu, Kylling, you know I love you and wish I could stay. But I made promise to you papa, and is important to always keep you promises."

I nodded.

"I know things hard now, but you parents love you very much. And you and you brothers going to be okay. I know dat. I know dat, always." She crossed her heart like Jenny and I do when we swear something is the truth. Then she hugged me tightly and gathered her bags.

At the door, Mom actually said Gunda really didn't have to go, if she didn't want to. "Theo will understand," she said. But Gunda said no, her leaving was for the best.

"Where to?" I asked.

"I have sister, Olina, in Rhode Island. I go there for now." She snuffled.

Before she closed the taxi door, she looked my mother in the eyes. "Don't make biggest mistake of you life, Claire. Sometimes mens do stupid things. But then is you job to say, 'Okay, you my husband. You stupid. But I forgive you anyway.'"

I don't think that's what Mom wanted to hear, cause she practically closed the taxi door on Gunda's leg.

"Bye-bye!" she said quickly, and stepped back to wave from the sidewalk.

As soon as we were in the front door, I burst into tears. "Why, Mama? Why did she have to go?" I cried.

I was shaking, and it felt like my body was burning up from the inside. Mom sat us down on the bench in the front hall and I crawled into her lap—as much of me as would fit.

It seemed like we were there for a long time. All that crying made my eyes sting. I sat up and looked into my mother's face. I wanted to ask her the big question even though I was afraid of what the answer might be.

But each time I tried, I couldn't get all the words out. "Are you and Dad going to get a . . . ? Well, since Gunda left, does that mean Dad's gone for g—? I mean, when is he coming back?"

I held my breath each time, and watched the tears cling to my mother's lashes and smudge her mascara.

"Everything's going to be all right," she said.

But she didn't look sure, Mud. Not at all.

I put my head back in her lap and just hung on. Hung

on until I fell asleep, and then it was dinnertime.

Since Gunda isn't here to cook for us anymore, we had spaghetti and tomato sauce from a jar. That's usually one of my favorites, but tonight I couldn't eat more than two bites.

As soon as I climbed into bed with Green Bean, I started crying again. Oh, Mud, do you think if my parents get divorced I'll turn into one of those girls who cry all the time? Haven's parents are divorced, and she cries at the drop of a hat, same as Lucia. Neither one of them has ever stayed the whole night at a slumber party. I don't want to be like that.

What's going to happen, Mud? I wish you could tell me.

Love,

Lorelei oxo

Word of the Day: *wary (adj.): on guard; watchful.*
"The zebra kept a **wary** eye on the hungry lion in the grass."

☺

Dear Mud,

Mom keeps asking me, "What do you hope to get out of the play, Lorelei?"

And I always give the same answer: "Well, I hope I don't stink up the joint."

The next thing I know, she's off and running about what it meant to *her* to be in *Peter Pan*. How she felt like she was finally home whenever she was onstage, and nothing in the world has made her feel that way since.

Blah, blah, blah. Can't she see I have a few other things on my mind?! I swear, I'm not having kids when I grow up. I don't want to be responsible for driving anyone crazy.

This afternoon's rehearsal was a humdinger. Mr. Blair made us do the "aura exercise" before rehearsal. It's where you're supposed to *feel* someone's aura.

Of course, first he had to explain what an aura is.

"It's a colorful field of energy that surrounds your body, people. Most of us can't see our auras, but it reflects the spirit you have inside you. It's part of what makes you who you are," he said.

He got a lot of *wary* looks for that one. Not that he cared. Just went ahead and paired us off. Luckily, me and Jenny were partners. Which made Veronica mad cause she got stuck with Curley Portis. (Ha ha! Hilarious.) The funniest combination was Paul Windsor and Saylor Creek. Mr. Blair said it would be a great exercise for Peter Pan and Captain Hook to learn how to work together.

So the exercise is you stand across from your partner and one person concentrates on a memory with their eyes open. Mr. Blair told us to think of something sad. Then the other person takes their hand and traces the outline of their partner's body, trying to get as close as they possibly can to them—*without actually touching them!* According to Mr. Blair, that's how you feel someone's aura and find out what color it is.

Of course, we were supposed to keep a straight face, which was impossible. At least for me and Jenny. We couldn't stop laughing and then we got the hiccups. Which made Veronica extra mad, since she was busy refusing to let Curley get his hand within a mile of her.

Paul was the only kid who had the hang of the game. As soon as he thought of something sad, tears spurted from his eyes. When it was his turn to trace Saylor's aura, he made the mistake of going down the front of her first. She thought he was trying to get fresh, and kneed him in the crotch.

Splat! Man down!

For the rest of rehearsal, every time Captain Hook came onstage, Peter Pan ran off. Not to mention, ever since we started doing these exercises, Drew, who used to sing perfectly on pitch, now sings off-key. And Jenny still sounds like Scarlett O'Hara.

Good grief.

Love,

Lorelei

P.S. I started to feel guilty after rehearsal today. I don't want you to think that just cause I was laughing during the aura game, I don't miss my dad anymore. I do. I miss him so much I can hardly think straight.

Oh, Mud, I wish you could tell me what he's up to. And I hope he knows that I love him with all my heart.

Wednesday, November 16th

Word of the Day: *menace (v.): to threaten.*
"Just for fun, Green Bean **menaced** Teddy's white rats and made them tremble."

⊘⊘

Dear Mud,

Jenny and *all five* of her sisters spent the night last night. I've never had a sleepover on a school night before. It was awesome. Even better than a sleepover on the weekend. Mom only let it happen cause Jenny's uncle was rushed to the hospital yesterday and her parents had to fly to Texas to see him.

Baby Jasmine slept with Mom, but the rest of us girls pulled out our sleeping bags and slept in the living room. We had the most excellent time. We made slice-and-bake cookies and a blanket fort, and played games until we were pooped.

Of course, Teddy was miserable with a houseful of girls. But he still thought it'd be funny to *menace* Jinger and Juliet with a story about twins getting sucked up our chimney in the middle of the

151

night. Twerp. It took forever to get the twins to sleep after that!

Jenny and I stayed up until the wee hours talking about clothes and boys and how we can't wait to be in the movies someday. And for a whole day I didn't think about anything sad. It was perfect, Mud.

But now they're gone and I realized it's been three days since Dad left. Where did he go? Do you think he misses us? He hasn't called to say hi or "I'm sorry" or anything, which makes me think maybe he doesn't miss us at all. Or love us as much as he says he does.

I was trying to remember the last time he *did* say "I love you," and I can't. I mean, I'm sure it wasn't that long ago, right? Cause he's my dad and that's what dads do: they love you to pieces. But I still can't remember.

So all day I've been trying not to think about that. Only the more I try to forget, the more I remember that I can't remember the last time he said it. It makes me feel empty inside. And there's something about feeling like there's nothing inside you that makes everyday stuff not matter.

Well, at least I have some really good news, for a change, so get comfy cause it's BIG.

Bo asked me to his house to study with him sometime!

Can you believe that? Of course I said yes, and we're going to try to do it this Saturday. Thank God I have a few days to figure out what to wear! And to convince Mom to let me go.

All this time I was worried he had a crush on Jenny, cause every boy in our class seems to. But if he likes me even a little, that would be tickety-boo.

So here's the plan: If we study together on Saturday, I'll finish all my homework on Friday, but not tell him I did. That way, when we're together, I'll seem really smart. *And*, if I'm too nervous to concentrate on our assignment (which I'm sure I will be), it won't matter cause secretly I'll already be done.

More later.

Love,

Lorelei ooxx

P.S. Uh-oh, I just realized Jenny's going to be really mad that Bo asked me to study and not *her*. Oh, brother.

Word of the Day: *ennui (n.): boredom.*

"If Veronica were my best friend, I would die of
ennui."

◎◢

Dear Mud,

Teddy, who gets mostly straight A's, has now declared
school a pain in his assterior.

For example, he got sent to Principal Sanchez today
for supposedly giving Matt Newsome the answers to
a pop quiz in English class. Only he never made it to
Sanchez's office.

Instead he cut and came home.

Anyway, *I* found out Teddy had cut school before I
got home cause Mrs. Gaines, the vice principal, called me
into her office and said, "Lorelei, do you know where you
brother is?"

"No," I said, wondering why grown-ups always think

just cause you're related, you automati-
cally know where your sibling is.

So she picked up the phone and

called my house. Mom answered.

"Mrs. Connelly, this is Seldom Gaines at Pinkerton. Is . . . um . . . Teddy at home with you?"

Turns out Teddy told Mom that just the eighth graders had a half day today and that's why he was home early. (I can't believe she fell for that!)

After dinner Mom told him he was grounded—you guessed it—for life.

"Yes, commandant," he said as his sentence was handed down, then saluted Mom like she was a general.

"Don't you dare sass me, young man," she warned.

"I'm sorry—I was just obeying you," Teddy said innocently.

But Mom knew that *he* knew he was sassing her with a capital *S*.

"Obnoxious," she hissed.

Teddy bowed. "Apologies," he said. Boy, he was pushing it!

"Go to your room," she ordered.

With that, Teddy moseyed extra casually upstairs, like everyone in the house filled him with *ennui*. When he was sure the coast was clear, I heard him and Happy sneak up to the attic. It seems Happy has taken it upon herself to bottle the beer Dad left behind percolating in those big buckets, remember? So while Happy bottled, Teddy smoothed on some of his homemade labels.

It seemed like as good a time as any to ask Mom where our sofa had gone.

"Your father came back to the house today and picked it up. He's just borrowing it for his new apartment until . . . well . . . we work things out." She sighed.

"So he's coming back soon?" I asked.

"I don't know. Maybe," my mother said, gloomy as could be.

I hate it when she gets like that. So I pretended not to notice. I just smiled my widest smile and said loudly, "Well, *I* know. I think you can work things out fine! Fine and dandy!"

"L-Lorelei," my mother stammered.

"Sorry, can't talk. I have homework to do," I chirped, and skipped away.

But the truth is, inside I felt antsy and wary, which for some reason made me think of Saylor Creek. I bet she feels antsy and wary all the time cause she never knows what's going to happen, or who's going to pick on her today. And you know what, Mud? For the first time I could see how not knowing stuff can make you mean.

I stopped in the living room and stared at the huge

empty space where the sofa used to be. I can't believe my dad came back and took it. Not even so much as a how-do-you-do. Just *yoink!* Give me the sofa!

As I turned to go, Green Bean came into the living room. She stood in the spot where the sofa had been and howled. Then she squatted and peed on Mom's antique rug.

"You tell 'em, Green Bean," I giggled, and tiptoed upstairs without mentioning the pee to my mother.

I just want to remind you that next Thursday is Thanksgiving, Mud. Which means we only have two and a half days of school next week. Hooray! And guess what. I asked Mom about going to study at Bo's house, and she didn't say yes, but she didn't say no, either. She said she'll talk to his parents and think about it.

"Maybe he can come over here instead," she suggested.

I admit that's further than I thought I'd get, but it's pretty much the worst idea she's ever had. I mean, for heaven's sake, we don't even have a couch!

I'm afraid if Bo sees how bonkers my family is, he won't like me anymore, and I already like him so much.

The only solution is to convince my mother to let me go to his house, where I bet it's quiet, and his parents are nice to each other, and nobody comes and steals the couch while you're at school.

Keep your paws crossed.

Love,

Lorelei xo

P.S. Why hasn't my dad called to talk to me?

Dear Mud,

No time for the Word of the Day cause I just came back from Bo's and I have to tell you everything before I forget a second of it!

I wore my favorite jeans, which I've never worn, but they're still my favorites cause they've been washed thirty-one times since I got them last summer and now they're supersoft. I also wore my apple-green socks with the Junior Mints on them, my pink high-tops, my favorite Calvin and Hobbes T-shirt, and that pink sweater with the green daisy buttons.

As I was getting ready, the phone rang. It was Jenny.

"What are you doing?" she said.

I wasn't sure I should tell her I was going to Bo's cause, like I said, I didn't want her to get mad at me. But if I lied and said I was going to the mall or something, she might want to come. And if I said no to that, then she'd *really* get mad. I had to tell her the truth. Most of all cause she's my best friend.

"Bo invited me over to study today."

Jenny got really quiet. So quiet that I could hear her swallow on the other end. I held my breath.

Finally she said, "When did he ask you?"

"Wednesday."

She made an *uck* sound. "Why didn't you tell me? I thought we were best friends!"

"Cause I knew you'd be mad!"

"That's stupid, Lorelei. I don't care what you do," Jenny laughed. But it was her fake laugh, I could tell. "Well, I have to go. My mom is calling me," she said, even though the only sound in the background was a faraway TV.

"Do you want to come over when I get back from Bo's?" I asked, extra nicely.

"I can't. I have to babysit my sisters."

"I could come help you."

"You mean, after you visit my boyfriend?" Jenny said snarkily.

"What are you talking about? Bo's not your boyfriend."

"So? I want him to be!"

"Well, I'm just going to study with him."

"No, you just want everything I have."

"That's mean, Jenny."

"*You're* mean!" she roared.

Tears wanted to skittle down my face, but I sucked them back.

"I have to go. Coming, Mom!" Jenny called.

"I can hear nobody's calling you," I said, keeping my voice steady.

"Yuh-huh."

Now I was mad.

"Jenny, it's not my fault Bo doesn't like you as much as me!" I yelled.

"Yes, it is!" she yelled back.

"No, it isn't!"

"*Is!*" And she hung up on me.

It was the worst fight we've ever had. But I had to get going to Bo's or I'd be really late.

Mom was out doing errands, so Happy dropped me off. Bo lives in a big apartment on Connecticut Avenue. The amazing thing is I've been passing by his building almost my whole life, and I never knew why it was my favorite until today. It's not just cause it's the prettiest one on the block, but obviously, deep down, I knew it would be important to me one day.

When we got there, a doorman in a gray uniform opened the car door for me and helped me out of the car.

"You must be Miss Connelly," he said, extending his white-gloved hand.

"Yes."

Then he raced ahead and held the door to the building for me, and walked me to the elevator. He leaned in and pushed the button for the fifteenth floor. "You're going to fifteen-A, Miss Connelly."

As the doors closed, he waved and told me to have a lovely day, like he really hoped I would.

I still can't believe he knew my name, Mud. But that settles it. When I grow up, I'm going to live in an apartment.

I got to ride up to Bo's floor all by myself. There was a mirror in the elevator. I smoothed my hair down and made sure my shirt wasn't tucked in too tight or too loose. I also checked to make sure I didn't have any boogers hanging out of my nose. And you know what? It's a darn good thing I did cause when I tipped my head way back, I could totally see one waving "Hallelujah!" from my nose hairs.

Thank God I had a Kleenex in my pocket and the elevator was really slow.

"Phew! That was close," I said to myself, just as the doors opened at the fifteenth floor.

Bo's hallway was wide like a hotel hallway and it

smelled like cookies. I stuck my nose in the huge bouquet of pink and yellow flowers on a long table by the elevator. They were fake! I've never seen fake flowers that looked so real, Mud. I felt them to be sure, and no doubt about it, the petals were cloth.

The walls in the hallway were painted dark green, and the apartment doors were shiny black. The carpet was dark yellow with gigantic pink roses on it, and when I stepped on it my footprint stayed behind. I didn't want to get it dirty, so I tiptoed along the edge as I snuck down the hall, around the corner, just to see what else was there. Nothing really. Another giant bouquet of fake flowers. And I noticed the numbers went from 15-A to C to D. No B. Weird.

The people in 15-C had the TV on. It sounded like they were watching football, which made me miss my dad. What's he up to, Mud? Can you make him call me? I know he's talked to Mom, but always when we're at school or in bed. Doesn't he know I miss him?

It sounded like somebody was practicing the trumpet in 15-D. They were pretty good, too.

But the cookie smell was coming from Bo's. I took a deep breath and knocked. "I'll get it!" Bo yelled. He answered the door wearing blue jeans, a white T-shirt, and a light-blue sweatshirt with a hood. It made his green eyes look like the glaciers we studied in earth science.

"Hi," said Bo.

"Hi. Where's B?" I blurted.

"What?" He looked confused.

"Where's apartment B?"

He smiled. "Oh, it's in here. I mean, my parents bought it and combined apartments A and B and then took the number off the door in the hallway so people would stop knocking on it. I know, it's kind of confusing when you first come."

"Not really. I just thought I'd ask cause, well, I knew there was a good explanation," I said, talking fast, turning red, and feeling dumber than a bag of string!

"Come on in. Cool T-shirt. I love Hobbes," he said.

"Me too."

The Emersons' living room is really big and sunny and white. White rug, white grand piano, white curtains and furniture. I figured it must have been brand-new since it was still so clean. And one whole wall was windows. I could see the tip-top of the National Cathedral in the distance. I've always thought it looks just like a castle.

Mrs. Emerson came out of the kitchen. She was tall, with dark, velvety-brown skin, long hair, and cocoa-colored eyes. There were pictures of her on the walls from when she was a model.

"Hello, Lorelei. I'm Kia. I'm so delighted to meet you," she said in an English accent. She came over to shake my hand. Her fingers were cool and slender.

"Thank me for having me. *No,* no, I mean, thank *you* for having *me,*" I spluttered.

"We'll be in the den, Mom," said Bo.

"Okay, I'll bring some cookies in, shall I?" Mrs. Emerson put a hand on my shoulder. "You do eat cookies, don't you, Lorelei? I just baked them."

"Yes," I said, mesmerized by the sound of her voice. I could have stood there all afternoon and just listened to her talk, Mud. I bet even when she's mad, it sounds beautiful.

I followed Bo down the hall to the den: another big room, all rusty red and creamy white, with furniture that looked brand-new, same as the living room. There was a spotless glass coffee table and a flat-screen TV in a giant cupboard with the doors open. On either side of the cupboard were wide wooden shelves that stretched from floor to ceiling, crammed with books and pictures of Bo and his family.

He plopped down on the red leather L-shaped sofa and immediately got swallowed up to his elbows. Eek! I didn't know where to sit, so I perched on the edge of one of the matching armchairs.

"Want to meet my cat?" Bo said.

He knelt down on the floor and lifted up the flap of red leather that made a skirt around the couch. "This is Six."

I peered into the darkness. There, staring back at me, was a black cat, with white on the tip of his nose and tail, and orange eyes.

"Aaaaw. Hi, Six." I smiled and reached my hand slowly toward him so he could sniff me. Right away, he licked my fingers and leaned his head into my hand so I could give his face a scritch.

Bo's eyes got wide. "Wow, he never licks strangers," he whispered.

"He knows I'm a cat person." I smiled, and thought of the way Green Bean had known the same thing about Lynn.

We sat up, and suddenly Bo and I were face-to-face. It's the closest I've ever been to a boy, Mud, and it made my heart stick in my throat and beat so hard, I was sure Bo could see it bulging out of my neck. Good grief, he's handsome. I wanted to reach out and touch his dark-blond curls. (Of course, I never would!) He smelled like the beach and clean laundry today. I could tell our moms use the same detergent.

Mrs. Emerson brought the cookies and milk in, and I jumped back to the armchair. She handed me a pretty plate with sunflowers painted on it, which I balanced daintily on my knees.

"Thank you," Bo and I said at the same time.

"You're welcome." Mrs. Emerson smiled, leaving us alone.

I broke off tiny pieces of cookie and nibbled them the way my mother does when we have company and she pretends she's not hungry.

"Food-shmood!" she'll say, and laugh.

But oh my, those cookies were good. Chocolate chip— my favorite. I could have eaten five. *Five*, I tell you! HA!

Suddenly, while I was in the middle of a ladylike sip of milk, Bo burped right in my ear, *"BUH-WAAAH-HHRRRRRP!"*

I looked over at him. He was bent in half with giggles.

"I can't believe you just belched like that," I snickered.

"I know!" He wheezed with laughter, then fell off the couch and bonked his forehead on the leg of the coffee table. "Ow," he hooted, which made me crack up and fall to my knees next to him. There we stayed until we'd laughed all the air out of us. It was the best, Mud. After that I wasn't nervous anymore.

"What's so funny?" a voice in the doorway said.

"Nothing. I—" But Bo couldn't get it out.

"He belched," I said, and we both howled again.

"I see." The man smiled.

"Lorelei, this is my dad," Bo said, out of breath.

"Hello," I croaked.

"Hello, Lorelei. Wyatt Emerson. It's a great pleasure to meet you. I've heard many good things."

"Thank you." I blushed. Wow, Mud, do you think that means Bo talks about me?

I stood up and collected myself as Mr. Emerson came over to shake my hand. He's tall, with a light tan, like my dad, wispy blond hair, and Bo's big green eyes.

"What are you two studying today?"

"Everything," said Bo.

Mr. Emerson patted Bo on the shoulder. "Well, you better get on with it, then."

"Nice to meet you, sir."

"Likewise, Lorelei."

I sat next to Bo on the couch this time and we took our books out. Even though I wasn't nervous anymore, I was really glad I'd already done my homework.

Bo's home is so clean, Mud, and it has all its furniture.

There's no fighting, or people doing things that make you want to crawl under the rug. Plus he has Six. I don't need to tell you, anyone with a cat is okay with me. And just as I was thinking about that, Bo and I heard loud singing from somewhere down the hall.

He covered his face with his hands. "Oh, no," he moaned.

"What's the matter?"

"My dad is singing!"

Sure enough, Mr. Emerson was wailing along to Prince.

"Purple rain. Pur-urple rai-ee-ain!"

"He promised he wouldn't sing while you were here," Bo muttered.

"I don't mind," I said, smiling. "I really don't."

Bo shook his head. He was positively miserable. I knew the feeling, Mud. I felt bad for him, but it also made me happy to see I'm not the only one with a mortifying family.

"Don't feel bad. You know what *my* dad did? He quit his job so he could make beer in the attic, and then a few days ago he kidnaped our couch."

Bo looked up and smirked. "He kidnaped your couch?"

"Yup. He and my mom aren't . . . well, just for now my dad's not living with us. So the other day he came back and stole the couch."

"Wow, that's lame," Bo said, trying to keep a straight face.

"You can laugh, if you want. It is pretty funny," I agreed, and we cracked up again.

Eventually, Bo and I went back to quizzing each other for our vocabulary test, and Mr. Emerson went right on singing to Prince. Then Mrs. Emerson popped her head in the doorway. "Bo, Jenny Owens is on the phone for you."

Bo looked at me. I shrugged, but my stomach did a belly flop inside.

What did Jenny want?

Mrs. Emerson handed Bo the cordless phone and left.

"Hello?" he said.

I didn't know what to do, but I couldn't just sit there. I got up and went over to the photos on the bookshelves. I could barely concentrate. In my head I could just see Jenny lying across her bed, twirling her black hair around her fingers, practicing puckering and unpuckering her lips in the long mirror on the back of her bedroom door. And giggling! She always giggles uncontrollably when she talks to a boy she likes.

I heard Bo say, "Lorelei's over and we're studying," as

I gazed up at a photo of the Emersons on a big sailboat in turquoise-colored water. They were all smiling and waving to the camera, and underneath the picture in black curly writing it said, "New Zealand."

"What are you talking about? Of course she's really here," said Bo.

Oooooooh! I wanted to scream! I don't know exactly what Jenny said, but obviously it was something like, "I thought Lorelei was kidding about going over to your house," and it made me hate her. Why does she have to be such a meanie? She didn't used to be that way.

I locked my eyes on the next photo: Bo in a white shirt and yellow overalls, wearing a pointy paper birthday hat. "My 3rd Birthday" was engraved on the bottom of the shiny silver frame. I giggled cause he looks exactly the same! Well, he's much handsomer now, but his smile is exactly the same.

Behind me Bo said, "I can't today. I've got a lot of stuff to do."

Aaaargh! My stomach flopped over again.

Next picture: Mr. and Mrs. Emerson on their wedding day, standing in front of a castle looking like the prince and princess who really live there. The black curly writing said: "May 18th, Bordeaux, France."

Bo: "I don't know. Clean my room. Wash the cat."

I turned around to look at him, and he rolled his eyes. I don't even know why he did it, Mud, but it made me like him even more.

I turned back. More pictures: the family at Christmas, the National Zoo, Disney World, visiting the Statue of Liberty. Bo dressed for different Halloweens: tomato, cowboy, vampire, ghoul, vampire. His finger paintings on all kinds of construction paper—framed!

I started to wonder, how come my mom never hung *my* finger paintings on the wall? She hangs all of Ryan's.

I picked up a photo of Six as a kitten, sleeping in a cereal bowl.

"Maybe . . . " Bo sighed behind me.

I froze. I didn't need to hear what Jenny must have been saying. I already knew. She was asking him if he wanted to go out with her sometime.

I had to swallow hard about ten times to keep the lump out of my throat, which is stupid cause I don't care if Jenny and Bo go out. (Well, I do a little.) What really bugged me was that Jenny couldn't wait to ask him. She just *had* to call while I was there, cause she was mad he'd asked *me* over to study and not *her*. Earth to Jenny: That's not my fault!

"Yeah, it's nice talking to you, but I really have to go," Bo said. "Okay, have fun at the movies."

He hung up. I slapped a smile on my face and turned around.

"She's kind of a weirdo. She laughs every other word and I can never understand what she's saying," he said.

"Yeah, she gets nervous, I guess."

"Whatever. She wanted me to go to the movies with her and Veronica this afternoon."

Veronica? Ooooooh, I can't believe Jenny! She told me she had to babysit.

"Really?" I said, as though I was barely listening. But all the spit in my mouth dried up.

"Yeah. I didn't know Jenny and Veronica were friends."

I nodded and went back to the couch.

Bo wrinkled his nose and laughed. "I wouldn't go to the movies with that dweeb and Jenny in a million years."

Oh, Mud, I wanted to kiss him! I didn't, of course. But I wanted to! Cause Jenny's little plan to get revenge on me, for I-don't-know-what, didn't work after all. Bo still liked me.

What an incredible day!

Before I left, Bo showed me his room. I thought it would be huge, but it's only a little bigger than mine. The walls are painted light blue, with sharks, whales, and eels on them so it looks like you're underwater. On the ceiling he has posters of Tiger Woods kissing a trophy and the Washington Redskins playing some team in the snow. He has a computer, of course. And then . . . he has his own phone shaped like a football, next to his own TV. Lucky!

But my favorite part was that one whole wall was an aquarium—a real one—full of fancy red, blue, and yellow-and-black-striped fish. Bo says Six falls asleep on his feet just staring at the tank for hours. Hilarious!

☯

I couldn't believe how fast three o'clock came. The only other day time zips by like that is Christmas. And I got to thinking: If I knew there would be plenty more days like this, I'm sure I could be brave and happy for as long as I needed to, no matter how crappy things got.

And *then* I thought, I bet God does it on purpose! The way She gives cats nine lives, I bet She gives people a certain number of days they wish would go on forever just so they'll be able to stand up to the ones they wish they could forget.

When I got home, I ran up to my room and started writing to you so I won't forget a minute of my afternoon with Bo. I didn't even stop to tell Mom anything. This is between you, and me, and Bo.

But if Grandpa were here, I'd tell him, too. I'd say, "Grandpa, I'm taking today as one of my reliving days. I had a fight with my best friend, but I made a new one. And it was better than I even imagined it could be. Today made me brave."

Mud, please tell God to tell my dad to call me, will you?

Love,

Lorelei xxxooo

P.S. I'm sure you've noticed that the red and blue ashtray I put on your grave isn't weatherproof. All the paint washed off last time it rained, and then Happy stepped on it by accident, and it broke. So I pinched the bird feeder from the dogwood tree by the side of the house and put that on your grave. Honestly, I don't know why I didn't think of it before. You used to spend hours sitting under that thing, watching the birds come and go. Well, now the birds can keep you company a little while longer. Just until I get to the garden store!

Word of the Day: *avert* (v.): *to prevent something from happening, especially something harmful.*
Also, to turn away.
"When the baboon mooned the hippo, the nun *averted* her eyes."

❧

Dear Mud,

As you know, Monday is my least favorite day of the week. Cause I have to wake up early after getting to sleep late on Saturday and Sunday. And I have five endless days of school ahead of me. Boring.

But this morning I was wide-awake at 5:22. Wide-awake and wondering what in the world I was going to wear. And what I should say to Bo when I saw him today.

Luckily, by 6:00 I had both problems solved. I  wore blue everything: blue jeans, blue socks with stars on them, blue polo shirt, and a blue sweater with yellow flowers on it. And I decided that after I said hi to Bo, I would wait and see what he said to me and then it would be easy to figure out what to say next. Phew! Crisis *averted*.

And this was just the beginning of another amazing day in the life of your pal, Lorelei Lee Connelly.

◯◯

I got to school early—really early—and went to the library to wait for the first bell. I was sure I'd be the only one there, but who should I see sitting on the floor, way in the back corner between the *V-W* and *X-Y-Z* bookcases but Saylor Creek! She was strangling a Coke between her thighs, and there were candy bar wrappers scattered around her as she sang along to something on her headphones.

I didn't know what to do. I didn't want her to see me cause she'd stop singing. But I also didn't want her to think I was spying on her by not saying hi. She's already mighty prickly. I decided to wave to her from the far end of the bookshelf.

"Hi, Saylor," I said. But she couldn't hear me. So I went up to her and tapped her on the shoulder, which startled her, and she almost slugged me.

"Hi," I said again, jumping out of the way in the nick of time.

"What do you want?" She scowled, removing her headphones.

"Nothing. I didn't think anybody else would be here this early, but then I heard you singing and . . . it's . . . Well, it's . . . I mean, you're the best singer I've ever heard."

Saylor cocked her head and sized me up with her good eye, while the drifty one focused on the books behind me. "Have you ever heard *West Side Story*?" she said.

"No."

"That's what I was singing. Here, listen." She handed me her earphones, which glistened in the fluorescent lights and smelled like Fritos. Gross.

But I put them on anyway, cause I didn't want Saylor to think I don't like her. Even though I'm not sure I do. On the other hand, why shouldn't I? Exactly. I don't know. I just haven't decided yet. But that's not the point. The point is, I got to hear this beautiful song called "Somewhere" from *West Side Story*.

In all the years we spent together on Earth, Mud, I can't believe we never listened to the musical *West Side Story*. It's so beautiful and terribly, terribly sad. Saylor says people die all over the place. Mostly of a broken heart. Surely they have a copy of it up in Heaven. I mean, don't they have everything up there?

Of course, Saylor sings "Somewhere" just as well, if not better, than the girl on the recording. I stood there speechless, thinking, God must have a plan for Saylor. Nobody sings like that for no reason, do they? Do they, Mud? It's a real question. I mean, God isn't playing a practical joke on Saylor, is She? Cause that would be about the meanest thing you could do to someone who sings like that and is already completely friendless.

"I'm glad you came back to *Peter Pan*. It'll be much better with you in it," I said, trying to be chatty.

"You already told me that the other day," Saylor harrumphed, and sucked on her Coke.

West Side Story was still leaking out of the plastic headphones that lay on the floor between us. Saylor pushed her limp hair behind her ears and burped.

"When Jenny does Wendy, does she sound like Scarlett O'Hara to you?" Saylor said out of the blue.

"You noticed that, too?" I gasped.

"Kinda!" she yelled ferociously. So ferociously, I couldn't tell if she was mad or happy or hungry or what. But then she laughed that deep, juicy, truck-driver laugh of hers that sounds like she dug it out of swamp mud, and I chuckled and breathed a sigh of relief. Until just as quickly Saylor quit laughing and said, "Why are you being so nice to me?"

"Why do you ask dumb questions like that?" I said, before I could think.

Saylor looked at me with her good eye, walleye focusing on my ear. "It's not a dumb question when you don't have any friends, stupid."

I'd never thought of it like that. "I see. Well, I guess I could be a jerk to you, if you want me to be," I said. Then wished I hadn't. Cause I wasn't trying to be obnoxious, Mud. Honest. I was just trying to figure out what to do.

Luckily, Saylor giggled—well, gurgled—and said, "Nah, that's okay." Then added, *"Jerk!"* so loudly, I jumped and braced myself against the bookcase.

I wanted to tell her to quit scaring me! But then I just started laughing along with her, cause it was kind of funny. Totally weird and funny.

The bell rang, which meant it was time for first period. Saylor crushed the Coke can in her fist and hid the candy bar wrappers between some books on the bottom shelf. She hoisted her backpack onto one shoulder.

"See ya, turkey," she said, and walked off.

Boy, she's an oddball.

☙❧

I have Miss Dove's English class first thing on Mondays. Bo does too, but I didn't see him in the hall on the way there. So I slid into my usual desk by the window. I was getting my stuff out when a voice said, "Can I borrow a pencil?"

I pulled my head out of my book bag and saw Bo standing over me, his dark-blond curls in a tumble. I tried to be cool, but it's next to impossible when your palms start to sweat and you can't stop grinning like a moron.

"Hi," I giggled.

Bo slid into the desk next to me that's usually reserved for Jenny. But Jenny and I haven't spoken since we had our fight, so I wasn't really saving it for her.

"Hi. Do you have a pencil I can borrow?" he asked again.

"Sure. What color?"

"Doesn't matter."

"Okay. Mechanical or regular?"

"What?"

"Do you want a mechanical pencil or an old-fashioned number two?"

"Uh . . . whatever." He shrugged.

"Right," I said, feeling stupid, stupid, stupid! What is wrong with me, Mud? This is when Teddy would say, "You see, you make everything into an international incident." Well, I can't help it! I mean, I don't mean to. I just wanted Bo to have all the pencil options possible.

"Here you go, dig in." And I handed him my pink pencil case.

"Thanks, this'll do." He pulled out a Ticonderoga. Then he spotted a Paper Mate. "No, wait. I love this kind. Can I borrow this one?"

He held up a mechanical #2.

"Of course. Those are my favorite too." I smiled.

"Yeah, they're good. You don't ever have to sharpen them."

"Exactly!" I practically shouted.

Haven, Audrey, and Sidney all turned around in their seats to look at me with stupid snicker-puss grins on their faces. I stuck my tongue out at them. Then I turned to Bo and shrugged, like *Ha, ha! I don't care!* And you know what, Mud? He laughed. A giant, bubbly I'm-on-your-side laugh. I think I love him.

When Jenny got to class and saw that her usual seat was taken, but that Bo was the one who'd taken it, she gave me a big best-friend wave and happily sat beside Haven.

But I wasn't buying it, Mud. Jenny doesn't get over a grudge that easily.

I waved back and all, but I added the stink-eye so she'd know *I* know she's up to something.

During lunch I found out what that something was.

She gave Bo my regular seat while I was feeding our science turtle, Lance Armstrong, and then she didn't save an extra seat for me.

When I came over with my lunch tray, Bo held up his hands helplessly. I felt bad for him. You could tell by the expression on his face that Jenny had duped him good.

"I'm sorry. I didn't mean to take your seat, Lorelei. Jenny said there was room for you, too," he apologized.

"It's okay. We only have fifteen minutes left anyway." I half smiled, as my face flushed bright pink. I wanted to die, Mud. Well, first I wanted to kick Jenny in the shins, then die and get sucked up by the linoleum floor.

I looked around and saw an empty chair at the mostly-eighth-graders' table. But I wasn't about to sit there. And there was a bunch of seats open at another table next to Jorge Peña (you know, the kid in my class who likes to set things on fire). No, thank you. And then I spotted Saylor, eating alone as usual.

I went over. "Can I sit here?" I asked, standing across from her, holding my tray.

"I don't care," she said, slurping her milk straight from the carton.

I sat down.

Saylor was surrounded by wadded-up paper napkins, and it looked like almost as much food was scattered around her tray as must have made it into her gob. Which makes you wonder: How come she's so fat if no food gets in there? Anyway . . .

"How's the mystery meat?" I said, just to be friendly.

"Sucks," answered Saylor, with a big sloppy mouthful of it.

It was gross. I had to tell her, Mud. "You know, you should chew with your mouth closed. Then maybe you won't have to spend the rest of your life eating by yourself."

Saylor stopped midchew and lifted her head, stringy hair dangling over the walleye. Fury in the other. "Do you really think that would make a difference?" she growled.

And honestly, I couldn't tell if it was a real question or if she was about to belt me.

I decided to answer like it was a real question.

"Yes, I do think it would make a difference. It's more polite to chew with your mouth closed, and people care about that stuff."

Saylor's good eye got big as a melon, which for some reason made me want to poke it.

"Maybe that's a good idea, *jerk*!" She laughed suddenly, and showed me her ABC food. "Oops," she gurgled, and clapped her hand over her yap.

Boy, what she really needs is a lesson on how to be less scary! But one thing at a time.

Lunch was almost over. Out of the corner of my eye I saw Jenny coming toward me with Veronica and Sidney beside her. They were giggling behind their notebooks.

"Lorelei, how can you eat over here?" Jenny said.

"What do you mean?"

Veronica pointed to Saylor. "Well, look what's sitting across from you."

So I asked her, "What makes you so mean, Veronica?"

And she put her hands on her hips and sneered, "What makes you such a nerd? Oh, I know. It's that you like to have lunch with other nerds."

She and Sidney cracked up, and all three girls walked off—even Jenny, who waved at me over her shoulder. I did *not* wave back. I looked right at her and kept my arms at my sides.

Bo came over to my table. "Hi, Lorelei. Hi, Saylor."

Saylor almost passed out.

"Hi." I gave a tiny wave.

"I really thought Jenny had saved you a seat," he said.

"It doesn't matter." I shrugged, even though it did. "I could tell you thought she had."

"Yeah, sorry. Want to walk to class?"

Oh my God, Mud! I almost choked on my sip of milk.

"Umm . . . sure." I coughed, and cleared my tray.

"Saylor, want to walk with us?" asked Bo.

She couldn't speak. She could only sit there and blink at him with her mouth half open. Finally she shook her head. "Nuh-uh," she glurped.

So we left.

@⁄⊘

Later on at play rehearsal, Mr. Blair made us do the "machine" exercise. That's where one person starts making a simple movement and sound, which they repeat over and over again, as though they're one part of a machine. A few seconds later another person in the cast joins the first person by touching their foot, or arm, or head, or back, and adds their own personal movement and sound, like they're *another* part of the machine. The exercise keeps going like this until everyone in the cast is part of the machine.

I wanted to ask Mr. Blair, "How is this going to help Drew Pembroke remember his lines? Or Curley stop missing his entrance?" But I guess he was just looking for things to do since Paul Windsor is out with strep throat.

So I was the karate-chopping part of the machine,

shouting "Hi *ya!*" with every chop. Saylor came up to me and jabbed me in the arm.

"Ow. Are you the jabbing part of the machine?" I asked her, annoyed.

"No, I'm this part of the machine," and she started cutting armpit farts.

It was pretty funny. But I noticed she was still looking at me. And she actually had a twinkle in her good eye.

"What?" I asked her between karate chops.

"I didn't even think Bo knew my name," she wheezed.

"Saylor, don't be stupid. Bo's been in the same class with us since second grade."

She stopped what she was doing.

"Yeah, but when you're nobody, you figure nobody notices you," she said plainly.

"Girls, stop talking!" Mr. Blair yelled at us from across the stage.

And we went back to armpit farting and karate chopping.

The truth is it's not like I didn't know what Saylor was talking about. Ask anybody in school, and they'd tell you she's a nobody. But she's wrong about one thing: They all know her name.

Which got me thinking: What do you suppose would happen if Saylor stopped agreeing with all those people who think she's a loser? I bet if she did that and chewed with her mouth closed, she wouldn't have to eat lunch by herself anymore.

Love,

Lorelei xo

Tuesday, November 22nd
7:10 A.M.

Word of the Day: *excruciating* (adj.):

1. extremely painful, either physically or emotionally.

2. intolerably embarrassing, tedious, or irritating.

"Dropping a brick on your big toe is not only clumsy, it's **excruciating**."

૭⁄૭

Dear Mud,

I just talked to my dad! He said he misses us a ton.

"I miss you, too. Why don't you come home?" I asked him.

"Well, your mom and I still have some stuff to work out."

"What stuff?"

"Oh, Peanut, it's complicated." My father sighed.

And, since I can't seem to hold anything in these days, I just said, "Is it about that woman? That redheaded woman I saw you with?"

Immediately I wished I hadn't asked that question, cause deep down I didn't really want to know the answer, which I

knew was going to be yes.

"No, it's not about her," said Dad.

"What?" Now I was confused. "But what about that big fight you and Mom had?"

"Sweetie, there's a lot of stuff I can't answer right now. Not because I don't want to, but because I just don't have the answers. What I can tell you is you're my girl and I love you to bits. I love you, I love you, I love you!" he sang.

It made me laugh. "I love you, too, Dad."

"And no matter what happens down the road, that's never going to change," he added.

What does that mean? I wondered. It's just like grown-ups to get your hopes up. Then freak you out with a sudden reminder that disappointment is right around the corner.

Teddy grabbed the phone. "Hey, Dad. Happy bottled all the beer up in the attic and I put labels on. Want me to bring some up to Aunt Lee's this weekend?"

"*No!*" hollered Dad, loud enough that Teddy had to hold the phone away from his ear.

"Okay, don't have a coronary."

Dad said something else. Teddy rolled his eyes. "Okay, I won't," he grumped, and handed the phone back to me.

"Dad, you're coming up to Aunt Lee's for sure, aren't you?"

"Of course."

"Hot *dog*!" I cheered. "Are you coming on the train with us tomorrow?"

"That's the plan," he said.

You never got to meet Aunt Lee, Mud. But you would have loved her. She lives in a huge house on her very own hill, which overlooks two other hills, in Merritt, New York. (That's right, "Merritt." Just like Dad's and Teddy's middle names.) The town is about an hour north of New York City. I looked it up on a map. Mom likes to tell people that Aunt Lee comes from the wealthy side of Dad's family. I don't know why she always does that—states the obvious. As though nobody is paying attention but her. It's *excruciatingly* irritating.

Aunt Lee is really my *dad's* aunt, which makes her my *great*-aunt, and if you notice, we share the name Lee. Dad says absolutely, I get it from her. But Mom says I get it from Marilyn Monroe's character in her favorite movie, *Gentlemen Prefer Blondes*, and it's just a happy coincidence that Dad's aunt shares the very same name. I say who cares?

Your soon-to-be-train-traveling pal,

Lorelei **LEE** Connelly

9:38 P.M.

Boy, you wouldn't think so much could happen between the hours of breakfast and dinner.

First, Dad came back while we were at school and took the dining room table and the toaster. He left the chairs, which look like a bunch of rejects at a school dance now that there's no table to pull up to.

When Teddy saw the situation, he came into the kitchen where me and Mom were. "How could you let him take our stuff?" he demanded.

"I guess he needed it." Mom shrugged as she took a box of mini pizzas out of the freezer.

"Well, we need it too!" my brother shouted.

All of a sudden, the air got sticky still. I looked up and saw Mom turn in slow motion to face Teddy. It was creepy. Her voice was low and dangerous, but clear as water. "Don't you dare mouth off to me. If you have a problem with your father, I suggest you take it up with him." Then she slammed the cookie sheet she was holding on top of the stove with an earsplitting *CLANG!* End of discussion.

Teddy and I skedaddled up to our rooms. When we were alone, I told him I thought he had a good point, and it wasn't fair of Mom to bawl him out just for asking a question, even if he did ask it a tad too loudly.

And you know what he said, Mud? "Thanks." Teddy actually thanked me. Which just goes to show you that even though he's my brother, he's not a complete waste of food.

☯

In other news, Ryan was suspended from preschool for "inciting a riot"—at least that's what the note pinned to his collar said. Mom said it's just Ms. Amarinda's overly dramatic way of saying my little brother doesn't play well with others.

I know what you're thinking, Mud: Ryan's the friendliest kid in the world.

Well, the trouble started last week when he announced to the world that he'd only answer to "Bob" from now on. If you forgot and called him Ryan by accident, he wouldn't ignore you, he'd yell, "My name is *BOB!*" till you were deaf.

Therefore, when Ryan/Bob led his classmates in a take-off-your-trousers-and-be-a-screaming-hippo contest at nap time today, Ms. Amarinda was plain fed up.

That's how my little brother got suspended from preschool and sent home with a note pinned to his person.

But if you think about it, it's not Ryan's fault. It's

Happy's. She's the one who renamed him Bob. So if the world were a fair place, Happy would pay the price somehow. And you know what, Mud? Sometimes the world is a fair place.

It's the only explanation for the FBI showing up at our house this afternoon looking for her. Not cause she renamed Ryan, of course, but apparently cause she's wanted in fourteen states and Mexico, for stealing people's everything.

"What do you mean?" asked my mother.

I was sitting on the living room floor where the sofa used to be, doing my homework, when the FBI arrived.

Special Agent Yo reached into his dark overcoat and handed my mom a photo. "Is this the woman you know as Happy Dinero?" he said.

"Yes," my mother answered slowly.

"Well, ma'am, her real name is Pearl Munson, aka The Polar Bear, for her ability to hide in plain sight, despite her size. She's head of the Lifters, a notorious international gang that has stolen over three million dollars. At least that we know of."

One hand flew to my mother's mouth while she stood there hanging on to the front door with the other. Freezing November air flooded the house.

"Is Ms. Munson here, ma'am?" asked Agent Yo.

"Yes," my mother whispered.

And with that, four men in black windbreakers with *FBI* painted on their backs in shiny yellow letters suddenly appeared at the front door. My mother let them in.

Minutes later, they were escorting Happy/Pearl through the house in handcuffs while Ryan clung with all his might to the leg of one of the agents, crying himself blue.

"Ma'am? A little help?" said the agent as they paused in the doorway. Mom pried my little brother loose.

Happy bent down so she was at his level. "Bob, dude, don't worry about me. It's okay. I'm going to be fine," she said.

And for a second Ryan stopped bawling. Then he cocked his head back, filled his belly with air, and wailed, *"What about BOB?!"*

Happy/Pearl latched onto Agent Yo and said, "Get me outa here!"

"Toodle-oo, Pearl!" Teddy called as he jogged down the hallway.

"Toodle-oo," I giggled, catching the one-eyebrowed nanny's dirty look, and off they went.

Mom closed the front door and looked at us with huge, miserable eyes. "Happy *Dinero*? Oh my God, how could I miss something so obvious?" she whimpered, holding her head on with both hands.

I thought she was about to cry. But instead, she let loose this deep, come-from-your-butt laugh. And *plunk*, she fell to her knees. Next thing I knew, we were all on the living room floor, rolling around like potato bugs, laughing ourselves empty. All except Ryan/Bob, that is, who was still upset. He stood over us, hands on tiny hips, and said, "It's not funny. I hope you all get eaten by goblin turds!"

"What? That doesn't make any sense," I chuckled. Too late. My little brother had stomped off to his room already.

What a day, Mud! What a day! I know I should be worn out, but I'm "full of soup," as Grandpa used to say.

Oh, boy, I can't wait to get on the train tomorrow. The only bummer is Dad won't be traveling up with us, after all. Now he's driving up on his own and he won't get there until Thanksgiving Day. But at least he's coming. And then we'll be together as a family again!

I just know that once Mom and Dad spend some time with each other, they'll be reminded of how much better it is when we're *all* together, and Dad will come right home.

How do I know these things, you ask? I just do. In

fact, you've probably noticed that I'm righter about more things than most eleven year olds.

Oh, Mud, now that you're gone, I feel terrible about leaving Green Bean here all by herself. I got down on the floor with her tonight and explained that Jenny, June, and January are coming over to feed her and play with her while we're away. And you know what she did? She reached out with her paw and touched my hand. It was like she was people and telling me she'll be okay. But would you check on her, anyway? You know, just to make sure she doesn't get too lonely? She'll know you're there. She's smart that way. And besides, everybody knows cats can see angels.

Your train-traveling chum,

Lorelei xo

Thursday, November 24th

Word of the Day: *harried (adj.): tired and annoyed.*

"No matter how much sleep she gets, my mom always looks ***harried*** these days."

⟨ oↄo ⟩

Dear Mud,

Today is Thanksgiving and we're at Aunt Lee's in Merritt, New York. I have my own room at the end of the hall with its own bathroom, so I don't have to share one with my smelly brothers, which makes me wish I could stay here forever.

The train from Washington was fantastic. I could ride it all day every day and never get bored. There are so many things to see. Junkyards and ragged neighborhoods with burned-out buildings sandwiched between whole buildings that have laundry hanging on the fire escapes,

 even in November. I always wonder, who lives there? How did the building catch on fire? And do the kids there ever get to ride the train that passes by

their window every day?

I like to stand on the jiggling metal platform between train cars, too. It scares me to death, but I force myself to do it. I stare down at the ground zipping by in a blur, while my heart rattles against my chest and my knees slap together, and I can practically feel the cars coming unhitched and me getting sucked under the wheels at one hundred miles per hour. *Squish! Zoom! Gone!*

The train to New York City was wall-to-wall people and suitcases. Everyone was chattering away like we all knew we were going someplace great and couldn't wait to get there.

Ryan and I sat together on one side of the aisle. I had him on my lap so we could both look out the window, while Teddy and Mom sat on the other side of the aisle. It wasn't until we got to Delaware that I realized none of us had mentioned Dad at all. It made me wonder if that means we're getting used to him not being around.

I know, terrible. But you know what's worse? That I didn't feel anything when I thought it. Not happy. Not sad. Just empty. Like there was nothing inside me. *That* was terrible, Mud. I had to change the subject in my head.

I'll read, I thought.

I parked Ryan by the window and stood on the armrest of the other seat to get my knapsack down from the luggage rack, when Teddy leaped across the aisle and said, "Hey, get your mitts off my backpack!"

First of all, I've never seen my brother move that fast. Second, I was barely touching his backpack. I had two fingers on it is all, so I could move it and get to *my* pack. Idiot. You're lucky you never had an older brother, Mud. They're freaks and they make stuff up.

When I said, "Calm down. I'm just getting my things," Teddy pushed me aside. "I'll get them for you," he snapped. It was nice of him, I guess, except he said it in such a mean way, it was hard to be grateful.

He handed me my backpack and grabbed his own, then sat down and cradled it like a watermelon. Suddenly he was on his feet again. "I'm starving. I'm going to the snack car."

"I'll come with you," I said, and he gave me a look like *Don't do it*. But I ignored him.

I knew my brother was up to something when Mom suggested he leave his backpack on the seat, and Teddy said sweetly, "I don't mind carrying it."

Why would he drag his two-ton pack all the way to the snack car, you ask? Well, I hope you're sitting down, cause you're not going to believe this.

When we were two cars away from Mom and Ryan, Teddy crouched and unzipped his pack. He pulled out a Tupperware container that had something white and wiggly inside.

No way! I thought, as Teddy opened the lid halfway and revealed Sid, his pet rat. I knew it was Sid, cause he has that black spot on the tip of his ear. I'm not kidding, Mud, my idiot brother brought his pet rat on the train to Aunt Lee's. All I could think was, *How is he going to get through life being such a knuckle dragger?*

Of course, poor Sid was going crazy, wondering what he'd done to deserve this punishment. Teddy clamped the lid down on him again, which sent Sid frantically poking his nose through the cluster of airholes that Teddy had punched in the plastic top.

My brother saw the worried expression on my face and got defensive.

"What? He's fine," he said, like *I* was the pinhead!

I wanted to sock him. Instead, I just stood over him and shook my head, blocking the other passengers' view of his precious cargo.

"Isn't it cool?" Teddy grinned, sitting on the floor. Then he poked me in the knee. "You better not tell Mom," he warned.

Now I had him. "Oh, really? Well, that's a pretty big secret you're asking me to keep. It's going to cost you." I narrowed my eyes like a gangster.

"That's blackmail," he protested.

I shrugged. "Call it what you want. You still don't have a choice."

My brother stood up, grumbling all the way, and tucked Sid's Tupperware carefully in the bottom of his backpack; then off we went to the snack car.

There was a line, so I had plenty of time to decide what I wanted. When it was our turn, Teddy stepped up to the ugly orange counter and whipped out a twenty-dollar bill he said he'd "borrowed" from Mom's purse, and got himself a hot dog in a soft bun, two candy bars, and some bright orange peanut butter crackers.

"For Sid," he said, wiggling his eyebrows.

He handed his money to the leathery old man behind the counter, in a crisp red and blue uniform, and gestured to me. "Also, whatever she wants."

The snack man nodded. "All right. What would you like, little lady?"

I liked his smile and his uniform's shiny gold buttons, which matched his gold name tag: T. RANDALL. I stood on my toes to see over the counter better.

"Twinkies and a large hot chocolate, please, Mr. Randall."

"Well, how do you do?" He laughed big. "What's *your* name, then?"

"Lorelei."

"Pretty name for a pretty girl. All right, Ms. Lorelei, Twinkies and a large hot chocolate comin' right up." He laughed again and leaned down to get his tallest paper cup.

Teddy got right in my face. "That's six bucks!" he squawked.

"Yeah, I'd say that's a bargain. I ought to charge you twice as much to keep Sid a secret." I smiled.

My brother rolled his eyes. But he knew I had him.

T. Randall arranged our snacks neatly in two cardboard trays, which he handed to Teddy. Then he gave me the change from the twenty. "There you go."

"Thank you. Happy Thanksgiving, Mr. Randall," I said, and tipped him two crisp dollar bills.

"Thank you, Lorelei." The snack man beamed and gave me the thumbs up.

Oh boy, Teddy was looking *harried* now. If there hadn't been people watching, he would have clobbered me for sure.

"Grifter," he said, jamming his elbow into my back.

"Ow! I don't know what that is, but I bet you I'm not one. What I *am* is an entrepreneur."

We found two stools at a high round table. Ugly orange, like the counter, and barely big enough to hold our cardboard trays, but right in front of the snack car's huge picture window. It was perfect, until the moment Teddy started to take Sid out of his backpack. What is *wrong* with him, Mud? If I hadn't shoved him into the men's room in the nick of time, he'd have fed his rat peanut butter crackers right out in the open—in front of T. Randall and the rest of the world. Ugh. I just wanted to sit by the window in peace and watch Pennsylvania go by in a bare, foresty blur.

☙

It took about three and a half hours to get from Washington to New York City. While we were in the cab going from Penn Station to Grand Central Station, all I could think about was poor Sid stuffed into the bottom of Teddy's backpack, in the backseat of a New York City taxi, missing his wife, Nancy, and wondering if this was the end. While Nancy was home, scratching her pointy little head and thinking, *Where the heck is Sid?*

The local train to Merritt wasn't as swanky as the Amtrak to Manhattan. It was a lot dirtier, and not as quiet, and there was no snack car. In fact, it was more like a city bus than a train. Most of the passengers looked worn out and read the paper, instead of looking out the window at the scenery zipping by. But not me. I like to see where I'm going at all times.

Aunt Lee met us at the station in her shiny black Rolls-Royce, like always. She's had that car longer than I've been alive, and it still looks brand-new.

As soon as we stepped off the train, Ryan said his throat was sore and he felt sniffly. Typical. He's such a baby. He knows if he's sick, Mom will give him extra attention. As if he doesn't get all her attention as it is!

But today she just patted him on the back and said, "You'll have to hang on until we get to the house." Then she climbed into the front seat next to Aunt Lee, and the two of them started gabbing away, Mom talking so fast she hardly breathed between sentences.

Aunt Lee is such a slow driver that twice cars passed us as we drove through town. But I like that she's poky. It gives me and my brothers a chance to gaze out the windows at the wide, tree-lined streets with mansions and crew-cut lawns on either side.

The last street we turned onto finally dead-ended at the stone pillars to Aunt Lee's driveway, which is about as long as the road from the train station itself! A brass plaque on one of the pillars lets you know in curly letters that you've reached Bethany Brook Farm, and below that, in square capitals, it says PRIVATE PROPERTY.

Aunt Lee used to live here with her husband, Miles Ward, who was a writer like me, and their daughter,

Bethany. But they're both dead now. So she lives in this enormous brick house with ivy growing up the walls, and a swimming pool, and a cemetery on her property, all by herself.

No kidding, Aunt Lee has an honest-to-goodness cemetery right in her backyard. Uncle Miles used to tell us stories about the family named Shamroy who first owned Bethany Brook Farm, back in the Civil War days, when it was three times as big and called Sunnyside. The Shamroy family gravestones dot the boneyard on top of the hill. And let me tell you, there are lots of them.

One day I want to bring my Ouija board up there and have a séance. See if any of those Shamroys have anything they need to get off their chests. Like which one of them was murdered? It's common knowledge that people were murdered left and right in the old days. Yes, indeedy, you'd just as soon get murdered as get a cold back then.

The two non-Shamroy graves in the cemetery belong to Uncle Miles and to Bethany, who died of cancer when she was only fifteen.

I never knew her. But Dad says she was his favorite cousin when they were kids. Aunt Lee has pictures of her all over the house. She was really pale and pretty, with long brown hair and sky-blue eyes. It's kind of weird to think if I were her, I'd only have four years left to live. And if Teddy were Bethany, he'd be dead by Easter.

⚬⁄⚬

Come dinnertime, Ryan's sniffles had multiplied. I guess he wasn't kidding before. So what? Still boring. Mom gave him some cold medicine with "Maximum Strength" on the box, and he was a zombie until this morning. It was delightful. The house was so quiet, it was like we forgot to bring him. By the time he came to, he was fresh as a pair of new underwear.

Unfortunately, things didn't go as well for Sid. Last night, our first night at Aunt Lee's, Teddy swiped a dinner roll and some grapes for him. Nobody saw my brother do it but me.

"Don't tell," he said later, while we were clearing the table.

"Okay, but that's a brand-new secret. It's going to cost you."

Teddy shook his head in disgust. Too bad. I now get to choose what we watch on TV for the next two weeks.

My brother and I snuck up to his bedroom while my mom and Aunt Lee put on their coats and took their wine onto the patio for some crisp Westchester air.

Upstairs in his room, Teddy dug the Tupperware out

207

of his backpack. It was empty. Sid was gone. Teddy turned his pack upside down and shook everything out of it, then felt around the bottom with his hands. No Sid.

He clutched his chest. "Oh, no. Where did he go?"

I guess my brother hadn't closed the lid on the plastic container very carefully last time he checked on Sid, which was on the train.

We crawled around Teddy's room on our hands and knees, quietly calling Sid's name, hoping with all our might that first of all, he *knew* his name. And second, that he'd made it from the Amtrak train to the taxi to the other train to the Rolls Royce to Aunt Lee's.

We looked everywhere. Under the radiator, dresser, bed, behind the trunk, toilet, sink; in the back of the closet. No Sid. So we widened our search to include the hallway, the linen closet, Mom's room, Aunt Lee's sewing room, and my room at the end of the hall. That's when we heard it.

Ruth, the cook, let out a shriek that made the little hairs on my arms stand straight up.

"Sid!" Teddy gasped in a panic.

We bolted for the back staircase. As we tumbled into the kitchen, we saw Ruth stalking a dark corner of the pantry. Her back was to us, but above her head, she hoisted a twenty-pound bag of potatoes.

"Wait!" Teddy yelled, but Ruth didn't even notice, and a second later she'd hurled the sack of potatoes to the floor. There was a heavy *thud*, followed by a muffled *eep*. Then silence.

If Ruth were a thing, she'd be a bowling ball with feet and arms. She teetered out of the pantry and reached for the counter to steady herself. She looked at me and Teddy sideways, her chest heaving up and down like the kitchen didn't have enough air for all of us.

"It was a rat! Did you see? A huge rat!" she panted.

"*My* rat!" Teddy cried, as his arms went limp and he slowly fell to his knees. Tears gathered on his eyelashes. He crawled to the pantry and lifted the sack of potatoes off Sid.

"Oh, no," he wept, coming out with his pet cradled in his hands like a wilted flower. "You can't be dead. You just can't," he whispered, and brought his friend up to his cheek. But Sid, whose whiskers were lifeless and his head at a right angle, was toast.

At that very moment, Mom and Aunt Lee, having missed all the commotion, came strolling down the hall, carefree as you please.

Aunt Lee was calling, "Ruth, I thought you were going to bring the coffee and—" But she cut herself off when she reached the kitchen and saw Teddy on the floor. "Teddy?

What are you doing down there?"

He held Sid up for her and Mom to see.

"Oh my God, a rat!" shrieked Aunt Lee, and quickly stepped back.

Mom went over to Teddy. "Teddy, where did you get that?" Her tone was firm.

"He's mine," Teddy said.

But Mom looked at me. "What?" She wasn't getting it.

"It's Sid from home," I explained.

Mom's hand flew to her cheek. "Oh dear!"

"*Oh, no!*" wailed Ruth, finally connecting the dots.

Even though you could tell my mother had a jillion questions, she didn't ask any of them. She just took a deep breath and got down on the floor with Teddy instead. There, she wrapped her arms around him and held him tight, down jacket and all. It was pretty cool, Mud. Pretty darn cool.

This morning there was a debate about whether or not we should wait for my dad to arrive before we had the funeral. But, for different reasons, neither Teddy nor Ruth liked the idea of keeping Sid in the freezer any longer than necessary, which means Dad has now missed *two* important funerals. I hope this isn't going to be a habit.

Ruth felt so guilty, she didn't want to attend either. But Teddy said he knew she'd killed his rat by accident and it would mean a lot to him if she would come and say a few words with the rest of us.

The morning was breezy and sunny as we all made our way to the cemetery. Teddy led the procession up the rolling hill, carrying Sid in his Tupperware. Mom and Aunt Lee steadied Ruth, while I had Ryan by the hand.

We Connellys dressed up like you would for a real funeral and wore the fancy clothes we'd brought for Thanksgiving dinner. Mom looked stunning in my favorite navy blue dress of hers and strawberry-red lipstick. She hummed "Taps" just like they play in the army.

Teddy had chosen a spot for Sid right between Molly-Anne Shamroy, who lived to be ninety-six, and Aunt Lee's daughter, Bethany, where Sid would have plenty of company, a view, and sunshine.

When everyone was assembled, Mom sang "Amazing Grace" as if she were back onstage at Princeton.

Then Teddy spoke. "I just want to say, Sid, you'll be missed. You were the best rat a guy could have. And I'm sorry you didn't get a chance to say good-bye to Nancy before your time came. I'll let her know you loved her and were thinking of her."

Teddy took a long breath and looked each one of us

in the eye. "Grandpa used to tell me that having faith is believing in something that you can't see or hear." He looked down at his hands. "I don't really know how you do that, but I'm going to give it a try because I have to believe that Sid is in a better place now. Even though I don't know why that place couldn't have been here, alive with me in Merritt. You'd have totally dug all the space and fresh air here, dude." Teddy paused. "I'm gonna miss you so much," he whispered as he laid Sid to rest in the moist earth. Then he turned away and wiped his face on the sleeve of his down jacket.

"Okay, somebody else go," he snuffled.

Ruth wanted to speak next. But she was too red-faced and wheezy to get the words out. Tears kept pouring down her cheeks, so we waited. Aunt Lee even handed her a fresh wad of Kleenex to hold over her nose and mouth to try to stop the flood. But nothing worked. Then Ruth got the hiccups. Urrgh, it was painful to watch, Mud.

Finally she caught her breath enough to say, "It was just a misunderstanding, Sid." *Hiccup.* "I'm *so* sorry. I'd give anything to take it back. Anything." *Hiccup.* "I hope everyone and Nancy, whoever she is, can forgive me. But I feel awful about what happened." Then Ruth wept up to the sky.

And guess what happened next, Mud. My brother, Theodore Merritt Connelly IV, reached out and put his arm around Ruth to comfort her. I saw it with my own eyes! It made me proud to be his sister.

After that, Ryan laid his mouse finger puppet that Gunda had knit him on top of Sid's Tupperware, and we each threw a handful of dirt on his grave. Mom sang the second verse of "Amazing Grace," and we walked down the hill so Ruth and Mom and Aunt Lee could start cooking Thanksgiving dinner.

☙❧

Later:

I'm up to my eyeballs full! My fingers even feel too fat to hold the pen! But at least I didn't throw up like Ryan. Seems he can't hold his pie.

Our Thanksgiving feast was *deeeelicious*. Four of Aunt Lee's friends came over to eat with us. (She likes collecting "strays," as she calls them.) And Ruth roasted a leg of lamb, as always, cause Aunt Lee hates turkey.

Dad arrived around 2:30. As soon as I heard his car in the gravel driveway, I ran outside to greet him. Oh, Mud, I was so relieved that I was happy to see him. When I hugged him, it was like all my missing him came rushing back and suddenly I couldn't hang on to him tight enough. He even had to leave his suitcase in the car and walk into the house with me hugging him and standing on the tops of his shoes.

Everyone was glad to see Dad. Even Mom, who couldn't help smiling from ear to ear when he came through the door. The grown-ups are still down there, with their coffee and brandy in the living room, yukking it up like old times.

I don't like to brag, Mud, but I knew if Mom and Dad saw each other and just spent some time in a place that made them happy, they would see how great it is when we're all together. I'm telling you, keep everything crossed, cause I have a good feeling about this.

I just have to mention one more thing. I keep thinking about Sid's funeral today. Not cause I miss him, really. He and I weren't that close. But when I looked at him in his tiny grave, all I could think of was you, Mud. And it made me miss you something awful. Like I realized for the first time that you're never coming back.

It's the loneliest feeling I've ever had in my life. It made me wonder if you can really hear me when I write to you.

Anyway, I know I've been asking a lot of you

lately, but keep an eye out for Sid, will you? Don't eat him! Just show him around. I'm sure he could use a friend.

Love always,
Lorelei xoxo

Saturday, November 26th

Dear Mud,

No Word of the Day today. I have too much on my mind.

We left Aunt Lee's a day early.

I thought everyone was getting along like lemonade and sugar, until last night I heard Mom and Dad fighting. I couldn't tell over what, but then a door slammed and Dad went out. He came back really late. And early this morning Mom woke me up and said, "We're leaving."

"Why?"

"Because we are. Get your things."

"But why?" I asked again.

"Because your father and I can't be here together."

I suggested Dad go home by himself. That way we could stay.

"Not an option. We are all going home together. If we go home separately, Aunt Lee will think that something

216

is wrong, and the Connellys do not air their dirty linen in public."

It's at times like this that I wonder what planet my mother lives on. How can she possibly think Aunt Lee doesn't already know something is totally wrong?!

But that's my mother. She's sure if she just doesn't say anything, everybody will think everything is perfect. I mean, I can see not wanting to "air our dirty linen" to strangers, but what about the people who love us? Isn't that okay? I wish I could find someone for my mother to talk to. She needs a Mud of her own.

I gathered my things.

Ruth packed us some sandwiches and homemade chocolate chip cookies, and we said good-bye to her and Aunt Lee, who whispered in my ear as she hugged me, "It's going to be okay."

But I don't know how she could say that, Mud. Cause everything seemed about as far away from okay as you could get.

We zipped along the New Jersey Turnpike. Mom wouldn't talk to anyone. So Dad just ignored her and sang along to Frank Sinatra on an old people's radio station. Annoying, cause he's a horrible singer. Not that he cares. He just opens his gob, and whatever comes out is fine with him. It reminded me of Bo's dad wailing along to

Prince. But at least Mr. Emerson can carry a tune.

Mom finally broke her silence and shushed him, and we played the alphabet memory game. Well, Ryan, Dad, and I played. Mom went back to staring out the window. And Teddy had his head in his Game Boy.

For all you biographers who don't know how to play the alphabet memory game, I'm going to tell you, cause you might find it useful one day when you're stuck in the car for hours and hours with your own unfunny father and two smelly brothers.

You start with *A*. Like, "*A* is for *aardvark*." And then the next person has to think of something that begins with a *B*, like *butthead*. But before they say it, they have to repeat what *A* was. So "*A* is for *aardvark*, *B* is for *butthead*," and so on, until you get to *Z*.

It's a good game cause you can say whatever you want. Silly stuff, gross stuff, as long as it's a real word and not a swear.

We were up to the letter *Q*, and it was Dad's turn.

He started, "*A* is for *armpit*. *B* is for *booger*. *C* is for *cootie*. *D* is for *dinosaur*. *E* is for *earwig*. *F* is for *fart*. . . . " All the way until he got to *Q*, when he said, "*Q* is for *quirt*," with a big fat grin.

I rolled my eyes. "Daaaad, it has to be real word. From the dictionary!"

Mom chuckled as she looked out the window. She still wasn't talking to any of us, but at least she seemed less mad.

"*Quirt*'s in the dictionary," said Dad.

"Yeah, right. You think you're funny, don't you?" I said.

He laughed. "What? I'm telling you, it's a real word."

"Sure, a real word in your head. I know you, Dad. You think if you smile, I'll fall for your baloney. But it's your smile that gives you away," I informed him.

He turned to Mom. "Can you believe this, Claire? My own daughter is accusing me of being the Avon lady of baloney peddlers."

But Mom said nothing. It was like she was trying her hardest not to have fun.

I leaned between the two front seats and turned my back to her.

"All right, Mr. Baloney, I'll bet you five bucks *quirt* is a made-up word," I said.

He looked at me sideways. "Oh, Peanut, I don't want to take your money."

"Well, I don't mind taking yours!"

Just then Teddy, never in a hurry to catch on, looked up from his Game Boy and said, "Did you say *quirt*, Dad? Good one." Then went back to gaming.

I faced my brother with a sinking feeling in my guts. "You know what that is?"

"Yeah, a quirt is like a short riding crop, usually braided."

I whacked him on the arm.

"Why didn't you tell me that before I bet Dad five bucks, you twerp?"

"Ow. I dunno, I wasn't listening." Teddy shrugged, obviously not caring one crumb about my life's savings. I was disgusted, Mud.

"Mom, did you know what a quirt was?"

She didn't answer.

I tapped her on the shoulder.

"Mom?"

She pulled her gaze away from the wet window. Outside, rain had started to fall hard. "What, sweetie?" she said in a faraway voice.

"Forget it. Never mind. Stupid game. Stupid everything," I muttered, and sat back.

I didn't even care about the five dollars, Mud. I just don't like being teased like that, where the joke goes on forever and you're the only one who doesn't get it. It's rude, I tell you.

Now rain poured out of the sky like God had left Her garden hose on. Dad could hardly see ten feet in front of him, so we stopped for milk shakes. Don't ask me how you get in a fight over something as happy and delicious as a milk shake, but that's exactly what happened.

I came out of the bathroom, and my parents were arguing by the cash register. It was mortifying. Everyone in the restaurant was staring at them. And the people behind my parents were like "Excuse me. Can you step aside, please? We'd like to pay our bill."

I wanted to die, Mud. D-I-E!

Teddy, Ryan, and I skedaddled with our milk shakes back to the car. Mom and Dad finally followed. Nobody said a word. It was horrible. We sipped in silence until the rain let up and Dad could get back on the road. He tried to apologize.

"Sorry about that back there." He smiled, like it was no big deal.

But it was way too late for sorry.

"What is the matter with you two?" I said.

Mom shook her head sadly, and Dad glanced at me in the rearview mirror.

"What do you mean?"

"What do you mean, what do I mean? You're ruining everything! Why did we have to leave Aunt Lee's early? Why were you fighting in the restaurant? What's going on?" I said.

Mom pressed her mouth into a thin white line.

"Tell them, Theo. It's your decision," she snipped.

"It can wait until we get home," Dad said grumpily.

"No, it can't. Tell us now," demanded Teddy.

Ryan, who'd been sitting between Teddy and me, just watching, handed me his milk shake and pulled the hood of his coat down over his face. I felt bad for him, Mud. He's too little to understand. I could tell he wanted to get away. We all did. But there was no place for us to go.

I looked out the window at the naked trees zipping by on either side of the highway. I usually love that part of the drive. But it's hard to enjoy anything when your stomach is tied into a double knot.

"Dad, spill it," Teddy said impatiently.

"All right. Well, I'm sure you noticed that things were difficult for your mother and me this weekend."

He glanced back at us anxiously, but nobody answered. He went on.

"Well . . . um. Your mother and I are not proud that we find ourselves in this situation. But it's clear we can't be together right now, and we've decided to separate. Officially. At the moment, it's the only way we can figure out how to move forward."

Teddy was furious.

"So that's it? You're leaving for good? Are you getting

a divorce?" he shouted.

His question startled all of us, even Mom.

Ryan started swinging his legs, kicking the backseat with his heels.

I picked at a thread at the top of my sock.

"Why aren't you answering me?" Teddy said.

"Don't you dare use that tone with me!" Dad barked. "Of course your mother and I don't *want* to get a divorce."

Teddy leaned forward right next to Dad's ear.

"But you're saying you could. It *could* happen. And you don't know for sure, do you?" he drilled. He sounded like Mom when she knows one of us is lying and she's just waiting for us to trip up.

My father gripped the steering wheel with all his might.

"Claire, I could use some help here."

But she didn't say a word.

Dad shook his head angrily. "Look, Teddy, it's too early to tell about any of that."

Teddy kept pushing. "But you have a hunch, right?"

"No, I don't. But—"

"But what?"

"But yes! I suppose anything is possible!" Dad admitted.

My heart stopped. Then started again, triple time.

"Is that true, Mom?" I asked.

"Yes," she said quietly.

Teddy sat back and crossed his arms over his chest. He was biting mad. I swear he could have jumped out of the moving car and I wouldn't have been surprised. Ryan tucked himself into a ball beside me.

After that I could see my father's lips moving, but I couldn't hear what he was saying. I don't even know how long the argument went on. All I know is I unraveled my whole sock.

When we got home, Dad didn't want to come into the house. He just dropped us off and left.

Mom and I went straight upstairs to our rooms.

I lay down on the bed with Green Bean, which is where I am now, and for some reason Grandpa popped into my head. Maybe cause I know if he were sitting here with me, he'd be telling me to look for the silver lining in everything that happened today. That's an expression: "Every cloud has a silver lining." It means, "Look on the bright side."

But it's a stupid expression, Mud. Cause clouds are just clouds and they don't have a bright side, which proves, once again, that grown-ups just make stuff up so they can talk to each other without actually saying anything.

Anyway, I've decided Green Bean and I should go live

with Bo and Six and Bo's parents. They're normal and happy, and his mom bakes cookies, for crying out loud. My mom can't even toast a Pop-Tart!

I wish you were still alive, Mud. I wish you were curled up beside me so I could hug you, and bury my face in your warm, soft tummy, and really truly talk to you.

Love always and forever,

Lorelei xoxo

Sunday, November 27th

Word of the Day: *nudist (n.): someone who does not wear clothes because he or she believes not wearing clothes is healthy.*

"The pig, with only a few wiry hairs, is the **nudist** of the barnyard."

❦

Dear Mud,

It's almost noon and the house is completely dead, except for me and Ryan, who came into my room at 6:30 this morning and stood by my bed. I figured he'd probably had a bad dream, cause he poked me and said, "What are you doing?"

"Sleeping."

"For how long?"

"A long time," I mumbled, hoping he would get the hint and go back to bed. But he just stood there staring at me. I could feel him. And then he started to hum! Aaargh!

I lifted up the covers and told him to get in.

"What's the matter?" I asked, as he snuggled up to me and Green Bean.

226

"Daddy doesn't live here anymore, does he?"

I raised up on my elbow and looked at my little brother. "Well, not for now, he doesn't."

Ryan lay on his back with his finger in the air, tracing the faint shapes of the glow-in-the-dark stars on my ceiling. "When's he coming back?" he whispered.

I got a lump in my throat. He's so little, Mud, and I could see he was trying hard to be brave. It made me wish I could say, "Tuesday. Dad's coming back Tuesday." But I didn't want to make a promise I couldn't keep. I think that's one of the worst things you can do to a person. So I told him what I knew and tried to sound as unworried as possible.

"I don't know when Dad's coming back. But we'll still get to see him all the time, even if he doesn't live here anymore."

Ryan eyeballed me and I threw on a big smile, hoping that if I *looked* like I believed what I was saying, he would too. But I don't think it worked cause he wrinkled up his nose like one of us had cut the cheese.

"What's wrong?" I asked.

He shrugged and looked away. Then he asked, "Will Dad bring us presents?"

"Maybe."

"Okay." Ryan nodded.

"Okay." I smiled and lay down, hoping he'd let me go back to sleep.

But a minute later he was poking me again. "Lulu, I'm hungry."

I gave up. We went downstairs and I made us one of our favorite breakfasts: waffle ice-cream sandwiches.

You take two frozen waffles and toast them until they're nice and crispy. Since Dad took our toaster, I had to toast the waffles in the oven. Then you spread one waffle with your favorite kind of ice cream. (For me, that's peppermint stick.) If you have some sauce—chocolate or butterscotch—and sprinkles, put those on top of the ice cream too. Then make a lid with the second waffle. Ta-da!

After breakfast Ryan and I watched cartoons and played go fish. While we were playing, I started to worry that all this stuff with Mom and Dad will wreck him. I mean, I'm eleven. I've had a lot of experience being brave. But Ryan's only four. He should get to be happy-go-lucky. Oh dear. What if he forgets how to be that wild, food-flinging *nudist* who drives us all crazy?

I wish I could make sure that doesn't happen, Mud. But the truth is I don't know how. And the double truth is sometimes I worry that all the fighting will wreck me, too. Like, maybe it's possible to be *too* brave, even if you're already eleven.

More later.

Love,

Lorelei xo

Wednesday, November 30th

Word of the Day: *rube (n.) slang term for a naive, unsophisticated person.*

"Bugs Bunny is a smartie and Elmer Fudd is a ***rube***."

◎◎

Dear Mud,

Why is it that the one day you want to leave early for school, nineteen things happen to make you late?

Since Mom hates to get up early and can't cook anyway, and Dad's gone *and* we're nanniless, I have to make breakfast for me and my little brother. Teddy's old enough to get his own.

So I wake up, shake Ryan awake, and while he gets dressed, I go downstairs and stick some Pop-Tarts in the oven, or slap some peanut butter on a waffle. By the time I have to leave for school, Mom's usually conscious and can take Ryan from there.

But this morning she was dead to the world, and Ryan came down for breakfast still wearing his pajamas.

"What are you doing, Squirt? Why aren't you dressed? It's not the weekend," I said, hurrying him back upstairs.

I barged into Teddy's room. He was at his desk.

"Teddy, can you help Ryan get dressed? I can't be late for school this morning."

"In a minute," he answered, turning off his video game.

"I won't tell Mom you were playing *Mortal Kombat* if you get Ryan dressed right now."

Teddy scratched his head. "How did you know I was playing *Mortal Kombat*?"

I rolled my eyes. "I'm not the *rube* you think I am, dingbat."

Gee whiz. It was barely after seven, Mud, and I was already harried. I stashed my little brother in his room and told him to wait there for Teddy.

He grabbed my sleeve. "Lulu, when's Daddy coming home?" he whined.

"Soon."

"When?"

"I don't know."

"When?"

"Ryan—"

"When? *When? WHEN?*"

"I don't know, *I don't know, I DON'T KNOW!* Quit yelling at me!" I shouted.

Of course he started to cry, which woke Mom up. She padded down the hall in her bare feet and bathrobe and stood in the doorway, bleary-eyed.

"I'm sorry I made him cry, but I don't know what his problem is today. And I have to go," I said before she could even open her mouth.

Then I raced down the stairs, grabbed my stuff, and left. If I walked really fast, I would just make the first-period bell.

To my surprise, I saw Jenny hurrying along only half a block ahead of me.

"Hey, Jenny! Wait up!" I called.

She stopped and waved. When I caught up to her, I could see she was upset.

"What's wrong?" I said.

"Everything. I hate everything."

"Me too," I agreed.

"No, get this. Not only is my mother pregnant, she just found out she's having twins. *Again!* She's a freak, Lorelei. My mother's a freak! So my parents want to move to a bigger house, which—duh!—our house is already way too crowded. But Dad says we can't afford a bigger house in our neighborhood, so he wants us to go to Texas. Texas! That way we can get a big house and he can be near my uncle at the same time. But I don't want to go to Texas! So he said"—Jenny lowered her voice like her dad's—"'Well, if we don't get a bigger house, then you'll have to share your room with three of your sisters, not just one, and I'm pretty sure you don't want to do that.'"

"Gee whiz."

Jenny turned around so she was walking backward. "The only good thing is Mom doesn't want to go to Texas either."

"That's lucky."

Jenny wiped away a tear that had pushed its way over her bottom eyelashes. "Yeah, but either way, my life is ruined," she croaked, facing forward again.

"Well, I have some bad news too," I said as we hurried along. Cause I figured, in a weird way, it would make her feel better to know she isn't the only one who wishes her life were different. "I think my parents might be getting a divorce."

"Oh, no," she gasped, and stopped dead, so that I walked right on by her and had to turn around and come back.

"Yeah, maybe."

"What are you going to do?"

I looked at her, confused. I didn't know I was supposed to do something, Mud.

"I don't know. There's still a chance they could get back together," I said.

Jenny grabbed both my wrists. "How can you be so calm?" she asked, panic in her eyes.

"I'm not calm! I'm just pretending to be calm by telling myself everything will be all right. Otherwise, I'll start crying and not be able to stop!"

"I know what you mean." Jenny nodded solemnly.

"Come on, we have to keep walking or we'll be late," I said. *I swear,* I thought, *we can't both burst into tears before school.*

We walked half a block in silence; then Jenny turned to me. "When do you get to see your dad again?"

"This weekend."

"Is he still stealing the furniture?"

I rolled my eyes. "Yes! The last thing he took was the TV in my parents' bedroom."

"You guys are going to be living in an empty house soon," Jenny snickered, and I snickered with her.

It made me happy we were talking like we used to. Cause even though I love writing to you, Mud, and I'll always tell you everything, you can't answer me. And sometimes I just want to hear if anybody thinks about the same things I do.

I was about to tell that to Jenny when she said, "Thanks

for listening, Lorelei. You're the only one I can tell certain stuff to."

"Ditto." I smiled, and we ran across the street before the light turned red.

We got to English class just as Miss Dove was closing the classroom door. We were pals all day. Even when Bo passed me a note in social studies class.

I was hoping Jenny hadn't seen him do it, cause we were getting along like we used to, and I didn't want anything to spoil it. But she was sitting right next to me. The good news is, instead of getting jealous, she whispered in my ear, "I told you he likes you."

It was a miracle.

Love,

Lorelei xox

Word of the Day: *catastrophe (n.) 1. a great, often sudden disaster. 2. complete failure.*

"Getting caught in a blizzard in your underpants would be a **catastrophe**."

☙

Dear Mud,

Something awful happened at school today. It was so bad and humiliating that I thought, *My life is over and it's all my fault.*

Then, out of the blue, something amazing happened to make it better. No kidding, you just won't believe it when I tell you.

The first part of the day was nothing to write home about, as Grandpa used to say. Which means it was boring, with a capital *B*. Everyone in the middle school play was just waiting for the 3:15 bell so we could go to our first dress rehearsal for *Peter Pan*. And yes, my mother

actually called Mr. Blair and asked him if she could come and watch! Thank God he said no.

When Jenny and I got to the

auditorium, Mr. Blair looked like he'd already been there for a while. His sleeve was rolled up and he was bossing people around, telling them where to put stuff, and trying to get the stage set cause he wanted to start at 3:30 sharp.

At 3:35 he gathered us all together, except for Curley Portis and Lucia Bowen, who were late, and told us how important it is in show business to be on time. Which makes you wonder why teachers always give that lecture to the students who already are on time, when it's the late ones who need to hear it.

Anyway, Mr. Blair said today's dress rehearsal was when we'd get to see how the play fits together: the costumes, the set, the music, all that stuff.

"Today, we'll finally get to see the whole puzzle. But this is a rehearsal, people, so you'll also need to be patient, which means being quiet. As in *no talking*." He parked his hand on his hip and looked directly at Veronica. "I can tell you right now, some things won't go exactly as planned. But that's what this time is for, to see where the glitches are."

And he sent us off to get changed. No dorky theater game today. Woo-hoo!

Miss Dove took the girls downstairs to one of the upper school classrooms that had been set aside as a dressing room, while it seems Mr. Melon was recruited to chaperone the boys in a second classroom down the hall, and to help Mr. Blair out in general.

As we trampled over the red and black floor mural of our school mascot, Boaz the Bull, I took Jenny's arm and whispered, "I wish Matt Newsome could see us right now, walking down his hall like we own it. He'd go berserk!" We chuckled and high-fived each other.

The costumes were already laid out in the "dressing room" when we got there. I don't know where Miss Dove found them all. But there were piles of them on the desks and hanging from racks.

My costume is beautiful. I get to wear a black-and-orange-striped leotard and tights—that's the Tiger part—and a green and yellow skirt made of light, floaty pieces of material that overlap each other at different lengths so they look like flower petals—that's the Lily part.

Veronica is the only one who brought her own costume. Her mom is a seamstress and insisted on making it herself. All I can say is, my oh my! When Veronica put it on and showed it to us, we couldn't believe it.

"Gracious me!" exclaimed Miss Dove, turning pink, like someone had just walked in on her on the toilet. Veronica was twirling around in the middle of the room wearing barely anything at all.

She reminded me of that Mitzi doll Aunt Glory sent me for Christmas a few years ago. Do you remember it, Mud? The doll's tag called her "Las Vegas Mitzi." She had long ostrich eyelashes, and a skimpy one-piece bathing suit made of purple sequins. You bit her feather headdress off as soon as I got her out of the box! Well, minus the headdress, Veronica looked a lot more like Mitzi than Tinker Bell, if you ask me.

"Uh . . . Veronica, I'm not sure that's what Mr. Blair was thinking when he imagined Tinker Bell's costume. But . . . I'm sure we can make it work. Somehow," Miss Dove muttered, quickly rummaging through a pile of clothes on the teacher's desk, until she found a gold cape and draped it around Veronica's shoulders, turning Veronica into a sourpuss for the rest of the afternoon.

After that, Jenny complained that her Wendy nightgown made her look fat. And Lucia (who finally showed up) burst into tears at the sight of *her* costume for Michael.

Practically the only person who didn't say a word was Saylor. She stood in a corner by herself, struggling into Captain Hook's billowy white pirate shirt with lacy frills down the front, and a long black coat with gold trim on the shoulders. Then she plopped down on the floor, where she pulled on a pair of high black boots, and smashed an already-squashed three-cornered hat on top of her head.

When she was dressed, she stood completely still in front of a mirror propped up against the chalkboard. She smiled and reached out, gently touching her reflection with one chubby finger, like she was just checking to make sure the person looking back at her was really her.

"You look great, Saylor," I said, not meaning to startle her.

"Muh?" she said, startled.

"I love your costume."

She looked down at the black coat in amazement and ran her fingers along the front of it. Her mouth twisted into a lopsided grin.

"Well, if you love it so much, why don't you marry it?" she snorted, and punched me in the arm.

☉⁄☉

By the time the girls got back upstairs to the auditorium, the boys were already there, razzing each other and running all over the place. Except for Paul Windsor, of course. He was at the piano practicing his scales. He sounded pretty good, too. You could hardly tell he'd had strep throat. Mr. Blair says it was Paul's love of theater that cured him so fast. And maybe that's true, cause he also didn't seem to mind that he looked like a girlie Kermit the Frog in his getup: green tights and ballet slippers, a green minidress with colored streamers sewn to the sleeves, and a little green beanie on top of his head. Boy, I bet he got beat up after rehearsal today.

We girls stayed in a clump until Veronica saw Hugh Knox, this ninth grader she has a crush on, and threw off her gold cape so she could parade around in front of him in her purple next-to-nothing. Dimwit.

Jenny and I were minding our own business when, out of the corner of my eye, I saw something that made my heart stutter and screech to a halt. Guess who was running the sound, Mud. Matt Newsome!

I almost passed out. "What's he doing here?" I whispered, clinging to Jenny.

"I don't know," she whispered back.

A second later I overheard Hugh razz Matt about the two of them having to "do time" running the lights and sound for the dumb-ass middle school play.

Matt laughed and said, "Yeah, I guess we wore out our welcome in detention."

Oh, great! I tried not to make eye contact with him. Cause even though he gave me The Nod when we were in detention together, you just never know with him. That's what makes him such a psycho. I turned my back, figuring if I pretended not to notice him, he wouldn't notice me, either.

Wrong. He came right over and stood behind me.

"So, Connelly, we meet again," he said in a deep, hoarse voice.

I whipped around, almost bumping into him. "Hi, Matt. What are you doing here?" I squeaked.

"We're your awesome stage crew," he said, and shared a laugh with Hugh and another boy named Pudge.

"Oh, great." I tried to smile.

"*Oh, great,*" Matt mimicked me. His friends laughed. "You better not screw up the whole play by sucking as Tiger Lily," he said as he poked me in the chest, which made all three boys laugh even harder before they shuffled off.

"Don't worry about me," I called after them, like Matt and I were pals and it was all a big joke. But good grief, my palms were sweaty.

"All right, people, let's gather," said Mr. Blair, now wearing a baseball cap with *Mame* written on the front. (For all you biographers, *Mame* was a Broadway musical and a movie musical, based on *Auntie Mame*, which was a book, a Broadway play, and a movie *without* music. How do you like that?!)

Mr. Blair said we all had to wait backstage in the wings, even if it wasn't our turn to go on yet, cause that's what real actors do in professional theater. Then he told

Hugh to turn out all the lights and make the stage completely dark. This is called a blackout, and it's when the actors in the first scene are supposed to tiptoe into place lickety-split, without making a peep. A few seconds later, the lights come up and the play begins.

But we didn't get that far.

During the blackout, Curley, who's playing Nana, the dog, ran into an armchair, cussed, then ran into Lucia, who, it turns out, is afraid of the dark and had just stopped, smack in the middle of the stage, crying and unable to move.

"Cut," said Mr. Blair, and Hugh turned on the lights.

Lucia ran off, bawling. And Curley confessed he can't see out of the eyeholes of his Nana suit, in the dark *or* the light, for that matter. Luckily Miss Dove had some scissors and made the holes bigger, while Mr. Blair assigned me to be in charge of placing Lucia onstage during the blackout.

We started over.

Everything was fine for about five pages, until Peter Pan made his entrance. He's supposed to appear in the big picture window and survey the Darling nursery. But whoever built the windowsill built it too high, and Paul couldn't get up onto it by himself. So when his cue came, all you could see was his ghostly white hand waving from the bottom of the window, like a tiny sailboat on the horizon.

"Cut!" Mr. Blair yelled again, and told Pudge to get a ladder. But the only ladder Pudge could find was pretty rickety, which meant he had to hold the bottom of it while Paul climbed up.

This time Paul appeared in the window and surveyed the nursery, like magic. He looked perfect up there in his Peter Pan costume. I started to get really excited about opening night.

Now, Mud, if this were Broadway, Paul would have leaped into the air and flown around like a fairy, tapping Wendy, John, and Michael lightly on their heads to wake them. But Mr. Blair said we can't afford the insurance to make anyone fly. "That's lame," Curley had said in rehearsal that day. And Mr. Blair had marched right over to him and set him straight. "This is theater, people. There's more than one way to launch a fairy." This afternoon, he gave the cue for Hugh to turn on the huge fan Hugh had borrowed from his dad's car wash and craftily mounted in the wings.

The plan was, the whoosh of air would lift and twirl the colored streamers sewn to Paul's costume, and that would make it look like he was flying.

Yeah, right.

The only thing it did was blow Paul backward, out of the window, like a giant split pea.

"Cut!" yelled Mr. Blair for the third time, pushing his Mame hat back on his head.

Luckily Paul fell right on top of Pudge, who was annoyed but not hurt.

And that's the way rehearsal went for the first hour and a half. Start, stop. Start, stop. Kids missing their entrances, singing off-key. Veronica threw a fit cause Mr. Blair finally told Miss Dove to sew her cape closed so the boys could concentrate on remembering their lines.

Finally, *finally*, we got to my entrance. I couldn't wait. I heard Miss Dove play my entrance music on the piano. I stepped onstage, Hugh turned the spotlight on me . . . and . . . Mud, I froze. It was awful, like somebody had stapled my moccasins to the floor.

My heart raced. *Just start talking*, I said to myself. But when I opened my mouth to speak, I couldn't remember my lines. Me! Lorelei! The person who knew *everybody's* lines only yesterday. I forgot *everything*. It was a *catastrophe*!

All I could think was, *Oh my God, I'm such a jerk. Matt Newsome was right, I am a loser and I never should have tried out for the school play in the first place. Never. Now it's going to stink cause of me. It's all my fault!*

Which made me think of all the other things that are probably my fault, like I should have tried to stop my dad from leaving on Saturday. Then we could be a family again and he would bring back the dining room table and the sofa. And Mom wouldn't be so sad all the time. But I didn't know how, Mud. I didn't know how.

Two tears scurried down my cheeks and dripped off my chin.

And if I was a better sister, I could have saved Sid, somehow. And I shouldn't have lied to Mr. Limeaux about my French homework today. I should have told him the—

Out of the corner of my eye I saw Mr. Blair approach the front of the stage. He was saying very loudly, "People, if you need a line, you have to shout out, 'Line,' so that we, or Mr. Melon, can prompt you."

I stopped crying. But my knees wouldn't stop knocking. I could feel everyone staring at me, waiting for me to do something. *Anything.* Finally I said, "Line."

Matt Newsome yelled from backstage, "Smooth one, Connelly! Very smooth."

"Quiet!" ordered Mr. Blair.

I wiped my face with the back of my arm. I kept waiting for my line. Waiting and waiting, but Mr. Melon wasn't saying anything. So I took a deep breath and hollered, "Line!"

"Pirates!" he whispered from the wings.

"That's it?" I said, looking in the direction of his voice.

I smacked my forehead with both hands. I couldn't believe it. I forgot one word, Mud. One stinking word! I wanted to scream, *Oh my god! I'm such a loser! A big, fat, stinky-butt loser!*

Now tears streamed down my cheeks. It was horrible. And then it got even worse when I came in late on my song and forgot the words to an entire verse!

I told you. It was a *catastrophe.* All I could think was, *This is punishment for every bad thing I've ever done in my life. I must be one of the worst people God knows.*

During a break, Jenny tried to make me feel better, saying everybody had been messing up. And even though that was true, I knew my mistakes were worse than anybody else's. I had such a headache. I wanted to be perfect, Mud. But I wasn't even pretty good. I wasn't anything.

෬෧

At the end of rehearsal Mr. Blair made some speech about how a bad dress rehearsal means you'll have a good opening night. But I doubt he's ever seen a rehearsal *that* bad.

I changed out of my costume as quickly as I could. Didn't talk to anybody. Didn't even stop to tie my shoes. As I was gathering up my stuff, Saylor came over to me.

"Hey," she said, chewing on a piece of her stringy blond hair.

"What do you want, Saylor?"

"I saw you screw up up there."

Across the room the other girls were giggling and whispering—I'm sure it was about me.

"Yeah, I know. Thanks for rubbing it in," I said, making it obvious I wasn't in the mood to talk. But she didn't get the hint.

She pointed to my sneakers. "You know, your shoes are untied."

"I know."

"Well, you should tie them."

"What do you care?" I snapped.

She shrugged and stayed put.

I admit, it seemed like she was trying to be nice. But she's such a weirdo, Mud. Chomping on her piece of hair, walleye cruising around the room, face all scowly.

"What do you want, Saylor?" I said, getting on the floor to tie my shoes.

"I used to forget songs and stuff too. But then I figured out how I could remember them. Do you want me to tell you?"

"Sure."

She looked surprised. "You do?"

"Yes. Quit being so annoying. Just tell me already."

She blushed and cleared her throat. Then she started

to explain in her rumbly he-man voice how she learns songs off the radio.

She said she doesn't memorize each word in the song separately. She learns the story of the song first, so it makes sense to her. After that the words come really easily. Plus, she said, the syllables of the words have a rhythm, which is kind of like a music all its own. A music that's separate from the notes in the song, even. And that's how Saylor remembers the song forever.

She said when she got the part of Captain Hook, she didn't know if the same technique would work for learning speaking lines, but she decided to try it. And I have to say, Mud, Saylor's the only one who didn't make a mistake in rehearsal today. She didn't even seem nervous. Which is pretty amazing for someone who's never been in a play before.

When she was done, Saylor punched me in the arm and left. Didn't say good-bye or anything. Just *sock!* and see ya.

What an odd fish. But I couldn't wait to get home and see if she was right about learning lines like that.

And you know what? She's dead right. I went over Tiger Lily's song, and when I thought of it as a story, I remembered it in a whole new way. I tried the same thing with my lines, and even some of Wendy's lines, just to test myself, and it works for those, too! Oh, Mud, maybe

I won't stink after all.

The funny thing is, if you'd told me this morning that today was going to be horrible, but by the end of it Saylor Creek was going to tell me something to make it a hundred times better, I'd have laughed and said, "That's impossible." Which got me thinking about other things that seem impossible.

I went downstairs to the kitchen and asked my mom about Dad leaving. I asked her how come she didn't try to stop him. And she said it's cause they'd decided together that his going away for a while was the best thing for the family.

"Do you miss him?"

"Of course," she answered.

"A lot?"

"Lorelei—"

"All I'm saying is you seem sad all the time. And if you miss him so much, then you should just tell him to come home."

My mother laid her hand on my cheek. "It's not that simple," she said.

"Why not? Look, Mom, if you're too embarrassed to tell Dad you miss him, *I'll* tell him for you. Cause I'm not embarrassed at all."

That's when she took me by the shoulders and told me

I'm a very sweet girl, and the best daughter she could hope for, but there's nothing more to be done at the moment. And even if there were, it wouldn't be my job to do it.

I'm not sure about that, Mud. Cause I do lots of stuff that's not my job, like taking out the trash when Teddy forgets and making breakfast for Ryan since we became nannyless. So maybe I should just go ahead and ask my dad to come home no matter what Mom says. Maybe that's what Jenny meant when she asked me the other day, "What are you going to do?"

Hey, I hope you ran into Sid and made him feel welcome up there. Just think how surprised he'll be. He'll never think of cats in the same way again.

Love,

Lorelei

Sunday, December 4th

Word of the Day: *eon (n.): an indefinitely long period of time; an age.*
"It took *eons* for the girl goose to get to Canada cause the boy goose gave her the wrong directions."

@/@

Dear Mud,

Me and my brothers are just back from a weekend with Dad at his apartment. It was weird. Not only that he has an apartment separate from our house, but that we have to make an appointment to see him now. We can't just show up. No, siree. Mom has to call and say, "This is when the kids are free." Then Dad either says, "No, that won't work," or, "I'm free too." And then they discuss who's going to drive us. "You should." "No, *you* should." And on and on. You'd think they were planning a school field trip.

Just before Dad came to get us, Mom went to the store to get milk. The thing is, we already had milk. So she wasn't fooling anyone. We all knew she just didn't want to see him.

Of course, the first thing he said when he walked in the door was

252

"Where's your mother?"

"She went to the store for milk." I smiled. Not a word more. But I knew he knew without my telling him what the truth was.

Dad looks different now. Have you noticed? He cut his hair short, like all-over chicken fuzz. And he was wearing blue jeans and sneakers. He couldn't wait to open his sport coat and show me his T-shirt that said *Alice Cooper: Hey Stoopid!* on it.

"Who's Alice Cooper?" I asked.

"He's a rock and roller. "

"Alice is a man?"

"Yeah. Cool, huh?"

Humph. I pointed to the word *Stoopid*. "He's not a very good speller."

Dad laughed. "No, he did that on purpose. It's a joke."

"Oh." I shrugged, not finding it that funny.

The truth is I was a little annoyed that it seemed like somebody had kidnaped my old dad and just plopped this trying-to-be-hip dad in his place. Personally, I like the father who wears faded khakis and button-down shirts and scuffy brown shoes on the weekends better.

Dad went to the bottom of the stairs and called for Teddy.

"What?" my brother yelled from his room.

Teddy announced yesterday that he didn't want to spend the weekend with our father and nobody could make him. But Mom said he had to go at least once. He agreed but, of course, he had to let everyone know how cranky it made him.

When Dad called for Ryan, he came running out of the den.

"Murgle pog," he giggled, and hugged our father.

"What was that?" Dad said, crouching down.

"Murgle pog."

"Use your words, buddy."

"Glerb, glerb, glerb!" Ryan shouted gleefully, and ran back to the den, waving for Dad to follow him.

But Dad just scratched his head and turned to me. "What's he talking about?"

I shrugged.

Dad tugged on his bottom lip, confused. "Hmmm . . ." he murmured as I followed him upstairs to Teddy's room.

"How's it going, Son?"

"Fine," Teddy mumbled, eyes glued to a video game.

"I'm going to check on the beer in the attic."

"Mm-hmm."

"Why don't you come?" asked Dad.

"No thanks."

"Sure?"

Teddy nodded.

"Why not?"

"Because I'm busy."

"Come on, Son, you can show me how the labels turned out."

That got my brother. He pushed back from his desk and led the way down the hall. He turned on the light switch at the bottom of the attic stairs and took Dad over to the corner where he and Happy had stored the beer.

Dad's face lit up like the Fourth of July. "Wow, dude, these labels look amazing. I love the lettering. Thank you," he said, and swallowed my brother up in a giant bear hug.

"Did you just call me *dude*?" Teddy asked.

"Sure," said Dad.

Teddy smirked. "That's funny."

And just like that, he and Dad were pals again.

Excuse me? How does my brother change his mind that fast? I mean, last night he didn't want to see Dad at all.

My brother and father spent the next twenty minutes gently loading as much beer as would fit into an old suitcase, so as not to "upset" it.

"Why don't you sing to it too?" I teased.

"Har-de-har-har," groused Teddy.

They lugged the suitcase out to Dad's car, then went into the dining room and took two chairs. Well, Dad already has the dining room table.

"Okay, kids, let's go."

"Spurg!" yelled Ryan, and dragged his Elmo backpack into the backseat with him.

Dad shook his head. " 'Spurg?' "

"Beats me," I said.

"All right, I'll figure it out later," he grumbled.

On the way to his apartment Dad let us stop at Dunkin' Donuts and get—are you ready? One dozen donuts, Mud. *And* he said we could eat in the car!

All right, maybe trying-to-be-hip Dad isn't that bad, after all.

Of course, Ryan went berserk from all the sugar. Even though he was pinned in place by his seat belt, his little arms and legs churned through the air like he was running some crazy race. The whole time he giggled and blathered on in his new made-up language. "Mergle ba nif? Spuggle ork goober moo."

As soon as we got to Dad's building and let my little brother loose in the lobby, he zipped around like a Hot Wheels car, yelling, "Frooby! Booby! Froob!"

It was funny *and* annoying.

"Jeez, I hope that's just the sugar talking." Dad chuckled.

⊘⊘

His new place is really nice, with tall windows that look out over the treetops, toward the Washington National Cathedral, just like Bo's. And shiny wood floors that make you want to slide around on them in your socks. He has pictures of us on the coffee table. Pictures that used to be in our living room at home. When do you think he mooched those? And do you think Mom knows? It's strange not to see any pictures of her anywhere. It's like he forgot something. It made me want to zip home and hug her.

There are only two bedrooms at Dad's. So he has one, my brothers share one, and I get to sleep on the big pull-out sofa. It's the same sofa Dad stole from our living room. And now I know why. Duh.

But, Mud, you'll never guess the best part about Dad's new home. Not only does it have a beautiful view like Bo's. It's right down the street from Bo's! I could walk there if I wanted to. Isn't that cool?

As soon as we got settled yesterday, Dad plopped us down on the stolen sofa and pulled a piece of paper out of his back pocket. He'd made a list for himself of things we could do over the weekend. Not amazing things like skydiving or waterskiing or going to a chocolate factory. But ordinary stuff you wouldn't think a person would need to write down, like going to the zoo or the movies, or watching a DVD. He even wrote down "eat lunch."

"Whatever we do, you're going to do it with us, right?" I asked.

He looked at me oddly. "Well, of course; that's the point."

"Okay." I nodded.

But it was a good question, Mud, cause the last time Dad was supposed to spend the day with us, I wasn't even eleven yet. And when that day came, he said he had to play golf with his boss instead. So Gunda dragged us to the museum, which was like going to school on the weekend! It was lame, I tell you.

Anyway, I'm sure that's why Dad made his list. It's cause it's been *eons* since he spent time with us and he can't remember what we like to do.

We decided to go to the National Zoo, which is just up the street from Dad's. It was really fun. And when it started to rain, we came back to his place and he ordered pizza.

We sat around the dining room table. Dad and Ryan in the two dining room chairs he pinched from our house, me and Teddy in two folding chairs that were a little too low, so I sat on the phone book. We dug in as Dad poured himself a glass of Connelly's Uncommon Brew.

He took a huge gulp. His eyes squeezed shut and his

mouth twisted into a pucker. "Oh, boy, that is the *worst* thing I've ever tasted!"

Teddy started laughing. As Dad reached for Teddy's Coke and drank half of it, Teddy took a whiff of Dad's beer. "Ooof! It smells like sour pee, dude." Dad shook his head, "I know. Something definitely went wrong with that batch," he said, and we all shared good chuckles, with Ryan adding a chorus of "Glurg! Moozle! Glurg!"

Dad leaned back in his chair and looked at Teddy. "'Glurg'? 'Moozle'? Do you know what he's talking about? When did this start?"

Teddy shrugged.

"I only heard him start doing it today," I said.

"Today, huh?" Dad got a faraway look in his eyes and a big crease in his forehead.

"Yeah, but he's just being an attention hog, like always," I said, pulling the cheese off my pizza.

Dad nodded, but the crease stayed right where it was. A few minutes later he turned to my little brother and said, "Well, Ry, as long as you're here, you're going to have to use your words." Then he brought Ryan a plastic cup of milk.

"Horp," said Ryan, and pushed the cup away. He hopped off his chair and shuffled into the living room to watch TV, which was fine until we broke out the last of the Dunkin' Donuts for dessert, and Dad said Ryan could have one only if he drank his milk and asked for his donut properly in plain English, not his ridiculous gibberish.

"Loop scrumble mimp," howled Ryan, and pounded his fists on the table.

"I guess you just want your milk and no donut, then," said Dad.

"Bork! Bork blam pog!"

But Dad ignored him. "Here you go," he said calmly, and set the cup down in front of my little brother once more.

I was going to remind him that Ryan hates milk, except for chocolate milk, and that's probably what he was yelling about, but I decided it would be more fun just to watch and see what happened next.

And it was a doozy! Ryan grabbed that cup of milk and turned it completely upside down. *Gush! SPLASH!* Milk everywhere. Then he reached into the donut box, snatched the last chocolate-glazed, and took a humongous bite out of it. I'm not kidding, it was like watching Wile E. Coyote skid off a cliff in slow motion.

Dad was around that table so fast, Ryan never even saw him coming. He dragged my little brother out of his chair. "Give me that donut. Give it to me," he demanded, and held out his hand.

Ryan shrugged and opened his mouth, and out plopped a giant glob of ABC donut.

"No, not the part you already ate." Dad was totally grossed out. "Give me what you have in your hand."

Ryan's eyes flooded with tears as he forked it over. I couldn't help thinking, *That's the difference between my parents and Gunda. They get grossed out over nothing, and she would have sucked the boogers right out of your nose if she'd had to.*

Dad picked Ryan up and held him at arm's length. "Ryan Clemmons Connelly, that was a *very* bad idea," he said in a low, furious voice.

"Humblegurg!" Ryan screamed at the top of his lungs.

"I told you to use your words!" hollered Dad, and tried to lower my little brother to the floor. But he refused to put his feet down.

"Pooooo! Poo-ooo-ooo!" he wailed, climbing up the front of our father.

"Stop it!"

"Zorg!"

"God, make him shut up!" begged Teddy, and stomped out of the room.

But Ryan squirmed and howled and still refused to put his feet down, so Dad lowered him to the floor, *into* the puddle of milk.

"Blaaaag!" screamed Ryan, and scrambled under the table over to my side. When he reached me, he stood up and hid behind my chair.

Dad leaned across the table. "This is my house, and you kids will do *what* I tell you, *when* I tell you," he said through clenched teeth.

Ryan trembled and bawled into my shoulder. *"Blob! Blah-ah-ob! Sned!"*

It was too much, Mud. I couldn't take seeing my little brother scared like that another minute. That's what I was talking about before—he's too little to have to be that brave.

I put my hands on the table and stood up. I wasn't sure what I was going to say, I just started talking.

"Dad, I don't know why you're being so mean. Ryan's mad cause you gave him milk and he hates milk, and he wants to know how come you don't know that. Even when he tried to remind you, you wouldn't listen.

"Also, you called his secret language ridiculous, which hurt his feelings," I explained.

Suddenly the air was completely still. No more crying. Hardly any breathing, even.

Dad looked from me to Ryan back to me. "You got all that from his . . . from those words he makes up?"

I nodded.

He gently leaned down. "Is what your sister says true, Ry?"

Oh, boy. I crossed my fingers, and inside my sneakers I crossed my toes, cause I wanted to be right, Mud. I *really* wanted to be right. Not in a snotty way, like Veronica, but in a good way, for my little brother's sake and so that everybody would be happy again.

Ryan finally nodded. "Mub," he said, sniffling and wiping his little red face on his sleeve.

Hallelujah!

"He says, yes, that's right," I translated with glee.

"I see. Well, I apologize for the misunderstanding. And . . . um . . . I shouldn't have yelled, either. I'm sorry." Dad said, looking pretty confused and exhausted.

"Quizzle froob flerb."

I translated. "Ry says he's sorry too."

Dad nodded slowly, but didn't say anything else.

The three of us cleaned up the milk, and Teddy came back, and we all watched a movie in the living room.

From that moment on, as long as I translated for Ryan, he was the sweetest, most well-behaved boy in the world. We could take him anywhere, which was never true before. Now I just think of him like a boy from another country, who's come to live with us and learn our language and customs and teach us about his.

Still, for the rest of the weekend Dad had this look on his face, like he was trying to solve a really hard math problem and couldn't.

◌◌

He dropped us off at home around four this afternoon. As soon as he was gone, Mom came running into the living room and hugged all three of us as though she hadn't seen us in a month.

"Ooooh, I missed you terribly," she said, then announced that as a special treat, we were going out for pizza. Can you believe that? Pizza twice in one weekend!

It was at the restaurant that Mom heard me talking to Ryan—him, gibberish; me, regular—and asked us what we were doing.

I told her, "Ryan's created his own language, and I'm the only one who understands it."

My little brother nodded in agreement.

Mom looked confused. Just like our father had, only with less worry.

"Mmm-hmm. Well, I'm glad you still like pizza," she said to Ryan.

"Zerp."

"That means he sure does," I translated. *"And he wishes we could have pizza at least once a week."*

Mom looked at me suspiciously. "Really? One word means all that?"

Ryan nodded vigorously.

"I see." She said slowly. Same as Dad. Boy, you'd think they could be together since they're practically the same person.

After that she didn't ask any more questions. The truth is, she was probably relieved to have the sweetest, most well-behaved four-year-old in the whole restaurant, for once, and she would have done anything to keep him that way.

More later, as things develop.

Love,

Lorelei xo

Word of the Day: *crabwise (adv.): sideways.*
"The crab parade marched **crabwise** down the boulevard."

◎◎

Dear Mud,

It's so late, but I had to write cause there's heaps to tell you.

For starters, I've been sick all week with a terrible cold and had to stay home from school. Luckily, I still got to go to rehearsal every afternoon, since one of Mom's favorite expressions is *The show must go on.*

Anyway, I'm 100 percent better now cause I had to be. That's right, I just willed that cold out of me. Every day, I would look in the mirror and say, "Hey, you stupid cold, I have a very important part in our school play on Saturday and I don't have time for you. Go make Teddy

sick instead."

And what do you know? This morning I was fine as fine can be. Just in time for opening night of *Peter Pan.*

The day started when I skipped downstairs to find Mom in the kitchen waiting for me. She'd made breakfast again. Yikes. Oatmeal. Ugh!

I leveled with her. "Mom, I hate oatmeal."

"No, you don't. You love oatmeal. Oatmeal is brain food. I used to eat it every morning before I had a performance, and I never forgot a single line in a single play. Oh, what an amazing time that was. All over campus, people I didn't even know told me to break a leg. *Break a leg* means *good luck* in the theater."

"I know; Mr. Blair told us." I stabbed at the lump of cereal in my bowl.

"There's nothing like the excitement of opening night. I thought I'd wear something special for the occasion," Mom said.

"Just wear something normal, please."

She pinched my cheek like a grandmother. "Don't you worry, I won't embarrass you."

Yeah, right, I thought. "I gotta go meet Jenny. We have to run lines and do some stuff, and then her mom's going to drive us to Pinkerton. So I won't see you until after the show," I said, and hurried out the backdoor.

◎◎

Oh, Mud, it was breathtaking. The auditorium was

packed. There were kids and parents standing all the way back to the metal doors that led outside. I was nervous, but in a good way. Until I saw Bo and his parents sitting in the second row, that is. Then I was a wreck! Oh, why did I peek through the curtain, Mud?

"Jenny, what am I going to do?" I whispered.

She took me by the shoulders, looked me dead in the eyes, and said, "It's opening night, Lorelei. Bo or no Bo, you have to go on and be great. That's your job."

The only other time I've seen her look that serious was when Mr. Big died.

"You're right," I said, and we hugged to give each other strength.

I was still nervous, though. Up until I stepped onstage and said my first line, and everyone laughed. Then it was amazing, Mud. I mean, all I said was "Pirates!" and they were goners.

I know, what's so funny about pirates, you ask? Well, if you think about it, a lot of things. But in this case it was the way I said it: surprised and a little annoyed at the same time. I'll bet you didn't know I could stuff more than one meaning into a single word. Well, it's just part of being naturally funny, I guess. Mr. Blair says nobody can teach you how to do that. You're just born with it.

And you know what else? Saylor got a standing ovation. No kidding. She came out at the end, and the audience stood up and cheered. It was fantastic. She totally deserved it. And luckily the clapping covered up the *rrrrip* of her pants splitting as she bowed.

The other amazing thing that happened is Matt Newsome almost missed a sound cue! Can you believe it? It was right as Tinker Bell drinks the poison. She's dying, and Peter is asking the audience to clap to bring her back to life.

In our version of *Peter Pan*, Mr. Blair gave Tinker Bell lines. But when he saw that Veronica can't walk and talk at the same time, he decided to replace most of them with an actual bell. (Oooo, Ronnie was mad!) And Matt Newsome is the guy responsible for ringing that bell.

So I was standing by myself in the wings, stage left (that's theater talk for the left side of the stage). And Veronica was lying onstage in her purple costume, like a dead crocus, while Peter Pan twirled and danced around, begging the audience to clap louder and save Tinker Bell's life.

Then, out of the corner of my eye, I saw something shiny whiz through the air and land with a *tink* on one of the armchairs that we use in the Darling nursery. I thought, *No, it couldn't be.* . . .

And right then, Matt Newsome leaned over the side of the catwalk (really just a ledge with a railing that's way up high backstage) and said in a loud whisper, "Hey! Can you hand me that bell?"

I looked where he was pointing his flashlight and saw that the thing that just whizzed past my head was exactly what I thought it was: Tinker Bell's bell! Matt had dropped it!

Now the audience was clapping wildly, and Peter Pan was looking pretty harried and pooped cause there was no ringing and Veronica still wasn't moving. So I grabbed the bell and zipped up the narrow metal ladder to Matt and handed it to him.

"Smooth move," I giggled when I reached him.

"Shut up," he hissed, and started ringing like crazy.

It was thrilling, Mud.

After everyone had taken their bow, Matt cornered me backstage.

"Hey, Connelly, thanks for helping me out," he said, greasy hair in his eyes.

"You're welcome. That was a close one, huh?" I smiled.

He grabbed my arm hard. "Listen to me, you little tweak, if you tell *any*one I dropped that bell tonight,

I will come to your house and string you up like roadkill. Do you hear me?"

I nodded. A second later, he let go and patted me on the back like we were pals.

Good grief, he's moody.

∽�‿∽

Downstairs, Mr. Blair gathered us all together in the girls' dressing room and said he was very, very proud of us. Then we all got opening-night T-shirts with *CATS* written on them. (Mr. Blair ordered *Peter Pan*, but they sent him the wrong show.) It didn't matter to us. We loved them.

Everyone changed out of their costumes and went upstairs to find their parents, except Veronica, who pulled a skirt on over her skimpy leotard and went to find Hugh Knox.

Jenny and I made our way through the crowd behind Saylor. But I'm telling you, so many people wanted to tell her how amazing she was as Captain Hook, they didn't even notice us. That's when Jenny suggested we wait and let Saylor go ahead, then start over. She's smart that way.

Poor Saylor didn't seem to know what to do with all those compliments. She hardly looked at anyone and just pushed her way through the crowd as fast as she could, as though maybe all those people weren't really talking to her.

Not Jenny and me. The second time we made our way through the crowd, lots of people said how good we were. And we said thank you to every single one of them.

Near the end, Bo tapped me on the shoulder, which took me totally by surprise. "Hi, Lorelei. You were really good," he said.

"Thank you." I blushed.

"You were good too, Jenny." He smiled at her.

"Thank you." She giggled and twirled her hair around her fingers.

Mrs. Emerson came over and leaned down to give me a big hug. She smelled like roses and vanilla, Mud.

"Lorelei, fantastic! You're a natural," she said in her fancy English accent. "And, Jenny, what a beautiful voice you have."

Mr. Emerson agreed, and then they took themselves off to the refreshment table, and Jenny went to find her parents. That just left me and Bo. I slung my hip out to the side, real casual-like.

"Were you nervous up there?" he asked.

I swatted the air with my hand. "Oh, heck, no. It was just like walking the dog."

"Really?" he laughed.

"No! I was petrified! I thought I was going to forget everything and totally stink up the play. But as soon as I got onstage and heard people laugh, I knew everything was going to be all right. And then it was weird: I was completely calm and excited at the same time." I grinned.

Bo grinned too. "Well, I thought you did a really good job. And you were *really* funny," he said.

"Thanks."

I watched him trace a square on the floor with his foot.

"What are you doing for Christmas vacation?"

"Nothing." I shrugged.

"Me neither. Maybe we should do some nothing together."

"Okay." I smiled.

Then he had to go. We said good-bye and went to find our families.

It was impossible to miss mine. Even though they were at the back of the auditorium, my mom was the only one wearing a fur coat and a party dress that went down to the floor. She promised she'd wear something normal! Ugh. If I hadn't been over the moon tonight, Mud, I'd have died of embarrassment right then and there.

"Not bad, squirt," said Teddy, and flicked me in

the head with his finger.

Dad lifted me off the floor in a huge hug. "Brilliant, Peanut. Just brilliant." He sighed, eyes sparkling. Smile as big as the Grand Canyon.

"Thank you," I giggled.

Teddy went off to find his friends. And another dad came over and started talking to mine about golf. I turned to my mother, who was yapping at Mr. Blair, and waited for her to notice me. Boy, she took her sweet time.

"It was fabulous, Noble. What you did with the kids was amazing," she gushed, and took Mr. Blair's hand in both of hers. "It takes me back to my time at Princeton when I played Wendy in *Peter Pan*. Did Lorelei tell you? I made quite a splash," she bragged.

Mr. Blair couldn't get a word in *crabwise*.

"I actually considered going into the theater, professionally, you know. Oh, how I loved it. It was intoxicating, that feeling of everyone on their feet, cheering when you take your bow." She put her hand on her heart and flashed her big party smile. "You know, I always thought I'd be a good director, too, because I'm very bossy." She laughed.

Well, that's the truth!

Poor Mr. Blair. His head was getting shiny. He obviously doesn't know that when Mom starts gabbing about her college years, you just have to interrupt her or she'll talk your ear right off. I had to help him. "Mom, how'd I do? . . . Mom?" I persisted.

She put two fingers under my chin. "Lorelei, please, I'm talking," she said, dropping her smile.

But Mr. Blair jumped right in. "You were super, Lorelei. Super-duper."

Jenny's mom and dad had joined the group by now. "Yes, you and Jenny were aces. You two stole the show," Junior said loudly.

"Ready for Broadway, huh, Noble?" Mrs. Owens guffawed and slapped Mr. Blair on the back.

"I'm sure they'd love that," he agreed.

All eyes were on my mother now, who finally said, "Yes, the girls were very good. You were very good, sweetie." She smiled and patted my cheek.

I waited for more, but none came. She just drifted off to talk to the vice principal, Mrs. Gaines.

I wanted to cry, Mud. I looked at Mr. Blair. He seemed like he was about to say something, but Veronica's mom came and yanked him away.

I looked for my dad, but he was nowhere. Teddy was with his friends. And Jenny's little sisters had her parents on the run. I didn't know what to do. I just stood there, all by myself with my heart in my sneakers, feeling like

I'd done something wrong, only I didn't know what. I wanted to go home, Mud. I decided, as soon as I found my father, I would ask him to take me home.

See? That's one good thing about having parents who don't live together: They always come in separate cars.

"Lorelei, can I talk to you a second?" a voice behind me said. It was Mr. Blair. He'd come back.

We walked to the front of the auditorium, toward the stage, where there were fewer people.

He put his hand on my shoulder and said, "I hope you know how wonderful you were tonight."

Suddenly all this air came rushing out of me, like I'd been holding my breath forever and was relieved I didn't have to anymore. I kept my eyes on the floor, though, cause I was afraid if I looked at Mr. Blair I'd start crying, and no way was I going to do that!

Didn't matter. He ducked down and caught my eye, anyway. "Listen to me—you're a fantastic natural comedian. Everyone was very impressed and proud of you tonight," he said.

"I don't think my mom was," I mumbled, then wanted to kick myself for having such a big mouth. I wasn't going to say anything, Mud. Honest. I was going to keep my feelings to myself like we Connellys are supposed to. But they just slipped out.

"Yes, I thought you might be thinking that. But I know your mother is proud of you too," Mr. Blair said.

"How? How do you know?" I had a big lump in my throat now, but I still didn't cry.

"I just do. The bigger point is, Lorelei, that when you know *inside* yourself that you gave your all, and did everything you could to do the best job you know how, it doesn't matter what anybody else says, or doesn't say."

That was it. I tried to hang on, Mud, but when I looked into Mr. Blair's light gray eyes, two tears zipped down my cheeks. Drat! *Drat!*

He smiled. "You have nothing to worry about, my dear. And tears? What tears? I don't see any tears."

I giggled cause it was like he read my mind. I dried my face on my sleeve, just as Saylor came over looking kind of sweaty.

"Hey, dude, my mom and dad want to say hi to you," she growled.

"Okay. Where are they?" I said brightly.

She pointed over by the punch bowl and cookies.

It's weird to think that even though Saylor and I have been in the same class since kindergarten, I've never met her parents. But even from a distance there was no mistaking her dad. He looks exactly like her. They're both "well upholstered," as Grandpa used to say. (Which means paunchy.) And Mud, he has the walleye!

Mrs. Creek looks just like a Cabbage Patch doll.

"Pleased to meet you, Mr. and Mrs. Creek."

Saylor's dad gave my hand such a squeeze I thought my pinky finger would break.

"Call me Filbert." He smiled, looking like he'd just eaten something sour.

Saylor's mom leaned in. "His name is Filbert because he's a nut. Get it?" She laughed.

"Oh." I smiled. But I didn't get it, Mud. I have no idea what she was talking about.

The four of us stood there looking nervous and dopey for a moment. Which made me wonder if Mr. and Mrs. Creek had really asked Saylor to introduce us, or if she'd just made that up.

"Did you like the play?" I said.

"Oh, yes." Saylor's mom sighed heavily, not sounding like she had. Then her eyes lit up. "That Jenny Owens was just wonderful, wasn't she? Such a beautiful voice, and my, oh my, what a slender, pretty girl."

"Sure . . . ," I answered slowly, waiting for her to say something good about Saylor, too. But she didn't. So I went right ahead and told Mr. and Mrs. Creek what I've been saying all along. That I thought Saylor should have played Wendy, cause she has the best voice of anyone in the whole cast.

And Mrs. Creek hooted and said, "Now, that's silly. Who's ever heard of a fat Wendy?"

My mouth fell open. I turned to Saylor like *You're not gonna take that, are you?* But it was weird—she wasn't even standing beside me anymore. She was standing completely behind me, as if I were a tree.

I looked at Mr. Creek to see if he would come to the rescue, but he didn't even seem to be listening. Just stood there, chewing on a toothpick and staring into space, walleye drifting around the room, same as Saylor's does.

It made me mad, Mud. But I didn't know what to say. I left to go find my parents.

When I saw my dad, I ran over and asked him if I could go home with him to his place tonight, and he said sure, as long as it was okay with Mom.

I found her still yapping about her theater days with a bunch of other moms.

I tugged on her sleeve. "I'm going to spend the night at Dad's. Is that okay?"

"Oh . . . all right," she said with a tight smile, then pressed her lips together like she had more to say but decided not to in front of her friends.

"Okay. See you tomorrow," I said cheerfully.

As I turned away, I heard Andy Butterfield's mom say, "Oh, no, Claire, are you and Theo separated?" And my mother answered, "Yes, for now," like it was no big deal, and probably just for the weekend. Oh, brother.

On the way to Dad's we stopped by the house; said hi to Mrs. Bixley, Ryan's babysitter; and picked up my pajamas and my journal. I *had* to have my journal. I also hugged Green Bean and told her I'd see her tomorrow. Then Dad and I hopped into the car and went to an all-night diner for pie. That's right, huge slices of blueberry and lemon meringue pie.

The whole time Dad talked about how much he liked the play and all the funny things I did. And I told him how I saved the day when Matt dropped Tinker Bell's bell. And he couldn't believe it. Then he said I'd been right about Saylor all along; she should have played Wendy.

Of course, I told him the mean thing Mrs. Creek had said when I told *her* Saylor should have played Wendy. And his mouth just fell open, like mine had.

"Poor Saylor," he said, and shook his head sadly.

"But why would she say something so awful?" I asked.

"I don't know, Peanut. I don't know. That's a question only Mrs. Creek can answer."

It was a great night, Mud. Even with all the weird, scary things that happened, I can't wait to get up tomorrow and do it all over again.

Lots of love and hugs and kisses,

Lorelei

XOXOOXOXOXOXO

Word of the Day: *unguent (n.): an ointment for soothing or healing.*
"The troll spread a pasty ***unguent*** over the boil on his forehead."
[***boil** (n.): a painful pus-filled inflammation of the skin.]*

⟋⟍

Dear Mud,

Ever since *Peter Pan* I've become pretty famous. Even some of the eighth graders know me, and not just as "Teddy's little sister." The boys call me "Connelly" and the girls call me "L.C." And they all ask me if I'm going to be in show business when I grow up.

"Probably," I say.

Which bugs Teddy like crazy. I don't know why. But I bet it's for the same reason it bugs Veronica: They're both jealous. Too bad there's no magic *unguent* for jealousy.

Love,
Lorelei

Sunday, December 18th

Word of the Day: *fribble (v.): to waste or fritter something away.*

"Instead of going to work, Mr. Lemon **fribbled** away the days polishing his rock collection."

☙

Dear Mud,

You better grab a snack and a cushion, cause I have a doozy for you today. We had another Dad day. So far we've spent more time with him since he moved out than when he lived with us. Sure, we used to see him every morning at breakfast or at bedtime, but that's not the same as actually doing stuff with him.

Today he wanted to take us to this little restaurant in Georgetown that serves breakfast all day. He loves that: breakfast all day.

We sat in a big curved booth. Dad ordered eggs Benedict and a side of bacon for himself, a grilled cheese for me, and a hamburger for Teddy. Ryan wanted ice cream. Since they didn't have his favorite (mint chocolate chip), Dad got him chocolate. I know, dessert

283

for lunch? It made me wonder if our father was buttering us up for something, cause Mom would never let that happen.

There was a glass full of crayons in the middle of the table. Our waitress, Venus, explained they were there for people to draw on the big square of paper that covered the tablecloth.

"Really?" I said.

"No joke," said Venus.

"Ziv," squealed Ryan, and dumped the crayons out in front of us and started drawing green fish.

When we first sat down, Dad kept checking his watch and looking at the door. When I asked him what was wrong, he said, "Nothing," and started talking about college football with Teddy.

So we were minding our own business, *fribbling* the time away, when this woman marched right up to our table, gave Dad a hug, and said, "I'm sorry I'm late! I had to park about a mile away."

"No problemo," Dad chirped and made room for her on the seat next to him.

The woman wore a black turtleneck under a short black jacket with brown leather patches on the elbows, and a long brown skirt over soft riding boots.

Teddy had no idea who she was. And Ryan barely

looked up from his fish drawings. But I couldn't take my eyes off her cause she looked familiar to me, only I didn't know why.

And then *BAM!* It hit me. She was the redhead I saw Dad with last month. Has he lost his mind, Mud? My stomach lurched sideways.

"Kids, I'd like you to meet Ivy," our father said, beaming.

The woman smiled broadly at us, took off her brown leather gloves, and stuck her hand out to shake.

She was about our mom's age. Her face was covered with golden freckles, and she'd twisted her red hair into a feathery bun.

"How you doin', guys?" she said.

Nobody answered.

Didn't matter.

"This must be Teddy," she went on, looking at my older brother.

He nodded and took one hand out of his coat pocket, shook hands, and put it right back.

"And you're obviously Lorelei. I hear you absolutely stole the show as Tiger Lily in *Peter Pan*. I wish I'd seen that." She smiled at me.

"Thank you," I said quietly, and glared at my father. Cause I wasn't falling for it, Mud—whatever it was they were trying to pull.

"And this little guy has to be Ryan."

"Farb moozle," he whispered, then dropped his crayon and hid under the table.

Dad leaned into Ivy. "I told you, he has his own language."

"Right, I remember." She nodded, amused.

I pulled Ryan onto my lap, and he wrapped his arms around my neck.

"What are you saying, little guy?" Ivy asked.

I translated. "He says don't get so close; strangers scare him."

"Oh, you don't have to be afraid. I'm a friend." She reached out gently to my little brother with long fingers that were pale and smooth. Her fingernails were painted sky blue.

Ryan buried his head in my sweater.

"That's okay. I'm sure we'll have plenty of time to get to know each other," she said.

What do you mean by that? I wanted to ask her. But the food arrived.

Dad and Ryan were the only ones who ate, though Ivy swiped a piece of bacon off Dad's plate and ordered some coffee for herself.

That's when my older brother turned to me and said, "Is she the redhead Mom and Dad had that big fight over?"

I gave a tiny nod. I couldn't believe Teddy was saying that out loud *in front of Ivy*!

"How dare you be rude to our guest." Dad frowned.

Teddy raised his eyebrows in surprise. "I'm sorry, but she's not *our* guest. She's *your* guest."

Oh boy, Teddy was asking for it. Not that he cared.

He leaned across Dad and said to Ivy, "I didn't meant to insult you, ma'am. I'm just trying to figure out who you are, since our parents don't tell us anything."

Ivy blushed but she didn't look insulted. She looked interested. She raised her eyebrows back at Teddy and patted his arm.

"Who I am, Teddy, is a good friend of your dad's. And since you all are the most important people in his life, I wanted to meet you."

"Well, what about our mom? She's an important person in his life. Do you want to meet her?" I asked.

Dad about choked on his eggs Benedict.

"I'd love to meet your mom. She's obviously raised three very intelligent children," Ivy replied without flinching.

"All right, you two, that's enough! You're being very rude. Ivy is not on trial here—she's just a good friend of mine who I wanted you to meet and spend some time with. Now eat, or don't eat, but show some manners.

Please," he added at the end.

We kids clammed up for the rest of lunch, while Dad and Ivy chatted away. I can't remember about what since I wasn't listening. I was singing "Tomorrow" in my head.

When we said good-bye, Ivy shook all our hands. Then she gave Dad a big hug and a quick kiss.

When Teddy saw that, he whispered in my ear, "Friends, my assterior!"

On the way home our father said how disappointed he was in our behavior. But he also said he realizes it's hard to be a child and go through as many changes as we have lately, and that maybe he should have warned us ahead of time that Ivy was going to join us.

"Nevertheless, I expect you to be open-minded, curious human beings who will make their best effort when they're introduced to new people and experiences, no matter what the situation.

"The Connellys are not dolts. Do you hear me? I want you to promise me you'll make an effort," Dad said, eyeing Ryan and me in the rearview mirror, and Teddy sitting next to him.

Teddy ignored him and kept staring out the window. Ryan muttered, "Glub," which meant, "Okay, I'll try."

And I said, "Okay," loud and clear, cause no way did I want to be a dolt. Not that I knew what one was before

I looked it up, but it sounded bad. And it is: **dolt** *(n.) a stupid person.*

Once we were home, Teddy and I decided not to tell Mom that Dad had introduced us to Ivy today. *What's the point?* we agreed. She'd just get mad. And we're not the ones she should be mad at.

Ryan, on the other hand, went on and on about meeting her. Turns out he kind of liked her. Go figure.

Of course, the whole story was in gibberish, so I was the only one who understood him. And when Mom asked me what he was saying, I told her he was blathering on about some sea monkeys we saw in a pet store window and now he wants some.

Ryan whapped me on the leg.

"Sherb! Pigglebum!" he cried.

Which means "You're a liar. That's not what I said!"

But I just smiled cause until he came out with it himself, Mom would believe whatever I told her. And today, that was what mattered.

I miss you, Mud.

Love,

Lorelei xo

Wednesday, December 21st

Word of the Day: *conundrum (noun): 1. a riddle whose answer involves a pun.*
2. anything that puzzles.
"How the lobster ended up in the tree was a **conundrum**."

☙

Dear Mud,

We started Christmas vacation today, and guess what. I got a postcard from Saylor. Now I know why she wasn't at school Monday or Tuesday: She was in Canada. I've pasted the postcard below:

Hi, Turkey. It's me, Saylor. I hope you have a good Christmas. I hope you get lots of presents. This is a picture of a Canadian moose. Don't ever come to Canada in December—it's freezing. Later, 'gator, Saylor Creek.

I know! I had to read it three times cause I couldn't believe it was from her. I mean, how come she's such a grunter when she talks, but her postcard is actually funny?

It's the same with her singing and her talking. It's a *conundrum*.

Also, guess what. We have a new nanny. His name is Shannon, although Teddy is refusing to call him anything until he's been with us for at least a week. He's such a lummox. Mom hired Shannon cause she said she wants to go back to work and she needs some "me" time to figure out what she wants to do. But Teddy and I know it's cause she's never had to be a full-time mother before and she can't take it. That's why we had Gunda . . . and Lynn, and Happy.

I liked Shannon the minute I met him. Not just because he's an expert at translating gibberish, like me. There's just something friendly about him. He said hello with a big smile. Not shy at all. And he's a good singer, too. He knows all the same Broadway songs Mom knows, and they were singing them together from the first day he was here, which put her in a really good mood.

He reminds me a little of Paul Windsor. The way they both walk and seem like they could be your sister. The difference is Shannon is super muscley and looks like Superman. So if he were in the eighth grade like Paul, nobody would dare beat him up after school.

Shannon arrived on Friday and took us to get our Christmas tree on Saturday; then he came home and put the lights on for us. He did a really good job, too. He didn't just lay them on the tips of the branches, like Mom does. He tucked them carefully inside, even at the back of the tree, which faces the wall.

I'm telling you, Mud, when you do the lights like that, the tree is so beautiful, you hardly need ornaments. Not that I'd ever say that out loud, of course. Mom would keel over.

Shannon made homemade blondies and hot chocolate and we decorated until the cows came home. By the end, you could barely tell there was a tree under all those ornaments. It should have made me feel happy and full of Christmas spirit, but instead I felt terribly sad cause I kept remembering you won't be here to sleep under the tree this year, Mud.

I wish you could come back just for that. I wouldn't ask for birthday or Christmas presents ever again if you could just be alive for one week each year. It would be our secret. And every night after everyone had gone to bed, I'd sneak downstairs and sit under the Christmas tree with you, and we could watch the ornaments twinkling in the white fairy lights the way we used to.

Oh, Mud, you have to promise not to tell anyone this, but when we decorated the tree on Saturday, I missed you more than I missed my dad. Do you think that's awful?

Well, it's the truth. I'm getting kind of used to him not being around.

I hope you find a tree in Heaven to sleep under, Mud, and that lots of angels come sit with you and keep you company. I couldn't bear the idea of you spending Christmas alone. But I figure Heaven is pretty crowded. Isn't it?

Love always,

Lorelei xoxoxo

Word of the Day: *barter (v.): to trade or swap.*
"The cowboys and Indians ***bartered*** guns for horses."

꩜

Dear Mud,

Merry Christmas Eve! I bet tomorrow is the best day ever up in Heaven. I can just picture it. Angels singing Christmas carols. All your favorite things to eat. And lots of presents for everyone, especially the children. Cause it seems to me if you're a child, and you're in Heaven, you died too young. Which means you wouldn't have had your fair share of Christmases on Earth, right?

Well, as you know, the Connelly tradition on Christmas Eve is that Teddy, Ryan, and I each get to choose one present from under the tree and open it after dinner. Of course, Ryan tried to *barter* for two presents, but he didn't have anything Mom wanted. All day I knew exactly which present I was going to choose, cause it wasn't for me, Mud, it was for you. Did you like it? I thought it was perfect.

You see, I had this hunch on Thursday that I should go to the garden store,

294

so I begged Mom to finally take me. I told the owner, Mr. Fogg, that I was looking for a cat statue to mark the grave of the best cat ever.

He said he thought he had just what I was looking for and led me all the way to the back, where they keep the Christmas trees for sale. There, next to a collection of stone rabbits and frogs, was a gray stone cat curled up like it was sleeping.

"It just came in yesterday." Mr. Fogg smiled.

"It's perfect," I said. "How much?"

"Twenty-seven dollars."

"Oh." My heart sank. "I only have seventeen dollars and fifty-six cents."

But I had an idea. "I usually get ten dollars for my birthday, right, Mom?" She nodded. "My birthday's not until July, but I could write you an IOU."

Mr. Fogg ran his fingers through his wavy black hair. "Hmmmm . . . You drive a hard bargain there," he said. "I'll tell you what: I'll give you the statue for what you have in your pocket, if you promise to put that ten dollars in the bank when you get it, and let it grow. Then we'll call it even."

"Deal," I said, and we shook on it.

I thanked Mr. Fogg at least ten times and told him he was making you and me both about as happy as a girl and her dead cat could be. And he chuckled and said that was the best news he'd heard all week.

I wrapped the statue myself, and could hardly wait the two days until I'd get to open it. I wanted to place it in the garden right away, and the moon and the back-porch lamp lent plenty of light. Mom and my brothers followed me out to the maple tree. Teddy took the bird feeder off your grave and hung it in the dogwood tree again, and then we had a moment of silence as I laid the sleeping stone kitty on top of your grave. Everyone smiled cause it was perfect, Mud. Exactly as I pictured it.

The four of us stood holding hands for a long time and agreed there would never be another cat like you. "He was true-blue," I said, licking a tear off my lip. And I swear, just as I said that, I felt like you were standing in the circle with us, Mud. It was amazing. I closed my eyes and I could practically feel your tail swishing around my legs. It was the best Christmas present ever.

As for tomorrow, I'm trying not to get my hopes up this year, cause anything could happen, what with Mom and Dad being separated, you know? I actually thought we'd split Christmas in two, and spend half of it at Dad's place and half at home with Mom. But she surprised everyone and announced that we would be spending Christmas Day as a family, like always. As in, *all together*.

So I'm trying to be ready for anything. The thing is it's really hard to feel prepared when you're not sure what's coming.

Green Bean is under the covers with me now. I've tried to get her to sleep under the Christmas tree all week, but she won't do it. She just sits next to it like she's waiting for something. And then it hit me. She's waiting for you, Mud. She's waiting for you to come back.

I felt terrible for her. I had to sit her down and explain that you're gone forever and you can't come back. Not even for Christmas. And while I was explaining, I started to cry. So guess what she did, Mud. She crawled up my chest and licked my tears. Sweet Green Bean. I love her up, down, and sideways!

Since our chat she's stopped looking for you. But she still won't sleep under the tree.

Sweet dreams, Mud. I hope you like the statue I got you. It's just my way of saying thank you and I'll never forget you.

Love always,

Lorelei xox xox

Word of the Day: *prowl (v.) to roam about stealthily.*
stealthily (adv.) in a secretive manner.
"Matt Newsome **prowled** the middle school hallways
looking for sixth graders to menace."

ↄⳠↄ

Dear Mud,

I hope you had a wonderful Christmas full of the
things you like most of all.

I got plenty of presents, as usual. If you were watching from Heaven, you know that Dad came over really
early this morning so we could open gifts first thing. He
and Mom sat on the floor with us, (cause we don't have
a couch, you know). And Mom sang along to her Christmas CDs while Ryan, Teddy, and I dug out from under a
mountain of presents, crumpled paper, and ribbon.

It was okay. I mean, I was relieved the day was off to
such a fine start. But our parents seemed kind of nervous,

 which didn't make any sense. *Cause they're
our parents!* And yet they sat side by side
and hardly looked at each other, like they
were strangers.

That's why it's doubly good that the new nanny, Shannon, arrived early too. Mom invited him to spend the day with us and he said yes, right away, cause he loves to celebrate Christmas with presents and carols and a great big tree. Only none of his friends do. They spend all day at the movies. So he said he'd be honored to join us.

When Shannon walked in the door, Ryan and I ran to hug him. He's one of those people who just brighten up a room. Wherever he goes, folks are glad to see him.

"Gloober!" Ryan shrieked, and clung to Shannon's leg.

"Hi, Shannon." I smiled.

"How are you guys?"

He had presents and ice-cream cake and champagne with him.

Mom, Dad, and Teddy came over.

"Well, I declare! Two people certainly think you're the best thing to walk through that door," my mother said with a tiny smile, and allowed Shannon to kiss her on the cheek.

Dad shook hands with Shannon and said he was really happy to finally meet him.

"Likewise," said the nanny, and handed Dad the champagne and ice-cream cake to take into the kitchen.

He turned to my older brother and nodded.

"Teddy," he said politely.

"Dude," Teddy replied, and they shook hands.

Then Shannon turned to Mom. "Claire, you're the only woman I know who can look stunning in her bathrobe at nine-fifteen in the morning."

My mother fanned her face with her hand. "You are such a smoothie," she gushed.

Dad came back from the kitchen holding a whisk. "You guys hungry?"

"Wheeeeg!" squealed Ryan, jumping up and down.

"All right, Connelly's Killer Waffles coming right up," he said.

"Need some help?" asked Shannon. Turns out the nanny used to be a chef, and he taught Dad a whole new waffle recipe. Mud, they were the best waffles I've ever had in my life. I stuffed myself silly.

It took breakfast and some champagne mixed with orange juice for Mom and Dad to start laughing and talking the way they used to. Then they really seemed to enjoy each other, and it was like Dad had never moved out at all. Therefore you can't blame Mom for asking him to dance when the song "White Christmas" came on.

Or for being confused when he said, no, he really had to start cooking the turkey.

"It can't wait for one dance?" she said.

Dad shook his head. "First it's one dance, then it's two.

Next thing you know, it's dinnertime, everybody's starving, and there's nothing to eat."

Mom tried to laugh it off by calling Dad "an old fuddy-duddy." But you could tell her feelings were hurt. Her cheeks were bright pink and she kept nervously tucking her hair behind her ears, even though it was already in a ponytail.

I looked at Dad like *Don't be such a jerk*.

And Teddy actually said, "It's Christmas. Why can't you just dance with her?"

But Dad wouldn't. He grabbed his coffee cup and went into the kitchen.

Teddy rolled his eyes. "I'll be in my room. I have some gaming to do." And off he went, taking the stairs two at a time.

Meanwhile, Mom stood frozen in the middle of the room. I didn't know what to do, Mud. When, out of the blue, Ryan stopped playing with his new Thomas the Tank Engine, marched over to her, and said sweetly, "Hizzle jub?"

Mom looked down at him and blushed again.

"I never know what he's saying," she confessed to Shannon.

"He wants to dance with you," the nanny and I said, at exactly the same time!

I thought she was going to burst into tears, she was so tickled. She took Ryan's tiny hands in hers and twirled him around the room.

It was beautiful, Mud. Of course, it didn't last very long, cause Ryan is four and has the attention span of a gnat. Not to mention he's *in love* with Shannon. So as soon as the nanny took one step toward the kitchen to help Dad out, Ryan ditched Mom, cried, "Blooooog!" and attached himself to Shannon's leg.

My mother looked embarrassed all over again, and I half expected her to stomp upstairs in a huff. I mean, who could blame her? But she didn't. She just smiled that tiny smile and said, "It seems this family would be lost without you, Shannon. Especially my youngest." She stroked Ryan's hair. "How wonderful that he's so crazy about you."

Shannon swatted her compliment away. "Oh, pshaw. Come on, let's go see if Theo needs help with dinner, shall we?" And he led the way into the kitchen.

Dad was hard at work making biscuits from scratch. All I could think was he must have felt really guilty for not dancing with Mom earlier, cause when she asked if she could do anything, he told her she could finish mixing his famous biscuit dough while he peeled potatoes.

I know, Mud, it seemed risky to me, trusting my

mother, who can't even make toast, to make homemade biscuits. But I decided not to say anything.

Everything was swell. Shannon and I were snapping beans while I told him all about the success of *Peter Pan*. Ryan was coloring at the kitchen table. And Dad was singing to the potatoes as he peeled them.

"Crap!" Mom cried, breaking the spell.

We all froze. Somehow she had misread the recipe and added twice as much butter to the biscuit dough as she was supposed to. It was ruined.

I knew I should have said something when I had the chance, Mud. I knew it! Now Dad was totally ticked off, and Mom felt terrible.

But Shannon didn't even bat an eyelid. He just rolled up his sleeves and said, "Don't worry about a thing," and made more biscuit dough, lickety-split.

Even my father was impressed. "Thanks, Shannon. Now, why don't you Connellys go back into the living room where you're out of the way," he huffed at me, Mom, and Ryan.

"But we want to help," Mom said.

Dad gave her the stink-eye. "I have plenty of help, thanks."

"All right, we understand when we're not wanted,"

Mom grumbled. She gathered up Ryan and me. "You know what you need, Theo? You need an apron that says GENIUS AT WORK. Then you wouldn't have to rub shoulders with hopelessly average people like your family." She smiled sarcastically and pushed through the swinging door.

Oh, brother.

As soon as we were in the living room, Mom seemed to forget all about Dad and was *la-la-la*-ing to "Jingle Bells" on the CD player. She even sat with us while Ryan and I played Candy Land.

Every now and then, she would look over her shoulder at the laughter coming from the kitchen, but she didn't say a word, Mud. Just hummed quietly and had this odd expression on her face. The best way to describe it is her lips were smiling, but her eyes were narrow slits, like she was a fox on the *prowl*.

When all the chopping, mixing, and mashing were done, Dad and Shannon joined us in the living room. They talked a mile a minute about baseball. Turns out Shannon is an encyclopedia of sports statistics, which was both impressive and boring at the same time.

When it was finally time for dinner, I suggested we lay a blanket out right next to the Christmas tree and have a picnic.

"That may be the best idea I've ever heard in my life."
Shannon grinned.

It was pretty brilliant.

So I went to find the biggest blanket we have.

We all got dressed up, like we do every year for Christmas dinner. Even the nanny, who changed into a chocolate-brown suit with a purple tie that he'd brought with him.

"Mom, why aren't you changing?" I said.

She just shrugged.

"Oh, Claire, I know you have something glamourous in that closet of yours. And every Christmas celebration needs a little glamour. Come on—I'll help you pick it out." Shannon smiled and offered his hand to my mother.

And what do you know? She took it.

A few minutes later the nanny came back down, followed by Teddy, and said Mom would be ready in a jiffy. With that, Dad started carving the turkey and putting it on plates in the kitchen, and Shannon, Teddy, and I carried them out to the living room.

Mom came down just as Dad was pouring the grownups some wine. She looked perfect in her high heels and red lipstick that matched her silk dress.

Even Teddy said, "You look nice, Mom."

Everyone agreed our picnic was the most beautiful thing they'd ever seen. I vote for having Christmas dinner like that every year, whether we get a new dining room table or not.

While we ate, Shannon quietly worked on drawing Teddy out of his shell by talking video games with him. Teddy was pretty impressed by how much he knew. But it was when he gave Teddy the lowdown on acquiring the ultimate weapon in *Final Fantasy* that my brother called the nanny by his name for the first time.

I wanted the day to last forever, Mud. But eventually Dad and Shannon had to go. Mom gave the nanny a hug and said, "I'm so happy you could join us today. Gracious, I don't know what we would have done without you. It seems there's nothing you can't do." Again, her lips were smiling but her eyes were slits.

Shannon blushed, and thanked us for having him. "It was the perfect Christmas," he said. Then he left with Dad, gabbing like they were old friends.

And that was my Christmas, Mud. I can't believe it was so much fun. My parents got along better than they have for ages, and Ryan didn't throw one tantrum.

Maybe that's cause Shannon was there, and everyone was on their best behavior. But maybe not. It could mean

Mom and Dad are thinking of getting back together. Then we'd be a whole family again. And Shannon could be our forever nanny!

I know. I shouldn't get my hopes up yet. But I have a good feeling about this. So cross all your toes.

Love, love, love,

Lorelei xoxo

Monday, December 26th

Word of the Day: *traitor (n.): a person who betrays his or her country, a cause, or another person's trust.*
"My mother is a *TRAITOR*!"

◌◌

That's right, Mud, she's a traitor with a capital *T*!

How perfect that my finger landed on *that* word in the dictionary today, cause I couldn't have chosen it better if I'd had my eyes open!

Guess what she did, Mud. Guess. She fired Shannon! She called him up this morning and said, "You don't need to come here anymore. Thank you."

"What are you doing?!" I asked her.

"After yesterday, he's practically best friends with your father. And I'm not comfortable with that," she said snootily, and walked away.

"That's crazy!" I roared.

But she didn't even look back.

So Teddy and I are refusing to speak to her. And we've decided we want to go live with Dad. Green Bean's coming with us, of course. Ryan, too. Poor little guy. He hasn't stopped crying all day.

Oh, Mud, what is *wrong* with everybody?!!

Your completely FURIOUS, UPSET, DISGUSTED, SOB-
BING, TIRED, CONFUSED pal,

Lorelei

Wednesday, December 28th

Word of the Day: *unfazed* (adj.): *not surprised or worried*.
"The rainforest monkeys were **unfazed** by the pouring rain."

୧⁄୧

Dear Mud,

Well, Teddy and I are talking to Mom again. We had to cause she refused to feed us unless we did. But yesterday we told her we want to go live with Dad.

Believe it or not, she didn't wig out. She just looked at us and said, "Not going to happen."

"Why not?" I said.

"Because you live here."

"But what if Dad wants us to come live with him?" Teddy argued.

She shrugged. "It doesn't matter what he wants."

"Well, what about what *we* want?" I demanded.

"I'm telling you, it's not going to happen," answered our mother, and left the room.

So what? Teddy and I agreed that we would ask Dad ourselves when we saw him today. And if he said yes, then that would be four (including Ryan) against one. Then Mom would have to let us go, cause nobody with a brain would pick a fight like that.

Teddy and I were happy to see that Dad was in a good mood when he came to get us. I mean, he did seem kind of antsy and in a hurry, but not in a bad way. More like he had a big surprise that he couldn't wait to show us. We got our coats and piled into his car. I sat in the front seat, and Teddy and Ryan sat in back.

When we were on the road, Dad announced he was taking us to McLean, Virginia. That's just outside of Washington, across the Potomac River. It's really pretty, with lots of trees and big old houses. You'd like it, Mud. There's plenty of room for a cat to prowl around.

"Why are we going to McLean?" I asked.

"You'll see." Dad smiled.

Teddy and I had agreed that I would start the conversation about our wanting to go live with him, and Teddy would join in when things got rolling. So I was keeping my eye peeled for the perfect moment. But Dad was such a motormouth, I could hardly get a word in crabwise.

Once I got as far as "You know that Mom fired our

nanny, Shannon, don't you?"

"Yes, she mentioned it. I thought she liked him," he said. And I was about to answer him, but he just went on as though there was nothing else to say on the subject. Irritating.

"Now kids, while we're out here in the beautiful countryside, I want to talk to you about something."

Even without looking at Teddy, I knew he was rolling his eyes. Seriously, Mud, do our parents think we're rubes? Whenever they start a conversation with *I want to talk to you about something*, it means it's something we don't want to hear! Not that that matters to them.

Dad cleared his throat. "I was driving around the other day thinking about change, because I know we've all been through a lot of it in the last couple of months and that can make you feel rattled. Which got me thinking about seasons and weather, and nature. And how, if the prehistoric sea creatures of ten million years ago had never crawled onto dry land and figured out how to survive, none of us would be here."

Teddy put his head against the window and pretended to snore, which made me and Ryan giggle.

"No, stick with me," said Dad, getting the joke but plowing ahead. "My point is, change is a part of life, right? But it's how you look at it that makes the difference. And the great thing is, once you understand that, you realize everything is actually fine. Better than fine."

I wanted to say, "If that's true, how come you're sweating?" But I didn't. And I had no idea what he was talking about either. None of us did.

"Dad, whatever you're trying to say, just spit it out," I said.

Suddenly, two deer zipped across the road. Dad slammed on the brakes and the deer galloped into the woods and zigzagged away through the trees. It was so startling and magical all at once. The four of us had to catch our breath, and no one spoke for a couple of miles. A light snow began to fall, and Dad pulled off the two-lane country highway onto a narrow gravel lane called Clover Dip. He put the car in park.

"Okay, as I was saying," he started over.

"Yeah, what's the bad news?" joked Teddy. But he was only half kidding, I could tell.

Dad turned around to face him. "That's exactly what I'm talking about. It doesn't have to be 'bad news.' It can just be news," he said cheerfully.

"All right already! Just tell us what it is!" I whined.

"Well, it's not just a *what*, it's also a *who*—"

He didn't need to continue. Teddy and I got it. We groaned quietly. "Oh, no—you're taking us to see

Ivy, aren't you?" I said.

Dad nodded.

"Mizzle swerb!" said Ryan, not even pretending to be bummed. Traitor.

Dad put the car in drive and we threaded our way through a forest of mostly pine trees. The tires kicked up tiny pieces of gravel that made a *rat-tat-tat-tat* sound, like bullets, on the bottom of the car, while the snow fell silently through trees that stretched so high, you couldn't see their tops unless you poked your head out the window. Teddy was slumped down in the backseat now, his arms crossed tightly over his chest. I'm sure that's why Dad reminded us that he expected me and my brothers to be on our best behavior for Ivy no matter what.

We rounded a corner, and the one-lane country road opened onto a wide clearing with a two-lane parkway and a traffic light. I swear, Mud, it looked exactly like a giant had grabbed a fistful of trees in each hand and just yanked them out of the earth so he could have a clear view.

I leaned forward in the front seat to get a better look at the sloping field that lay across the road and to the left of us. In the middle of the field stood a brick house with white columns like a prize at the end of its twisting driveway. It was beautiful, Mud. When I grow up, I'm going to live in a house just like that.

We turned left onto the parkway and waited for the light to turn green. There was a gas station, and a pretty block of stores straight ahead such as a dry cleaner's, a knitting shop, an antique shop, and a country store.

Dad pulled into the grass and gravel parking lot of the country store. It looked more like a big log shack, really. The outside was painted dark green and it had a blue door, but the paint was peeling off both. If it hadn't had a wooden bench on the porch and curtains in the windows, you'd have wondered if it was even open.

"Here we are. Home of the best ice cream in the whole wide world!" Dad announced as he stopped the car.

The sign hanging off the roof over the porch read ESTHER'S GENERAL STORE. FRESH LOCAL VEGETABLES, TRIPLE-DECKER SANDWICHES, AND HOMEMADE ICE CREAM.

"Come on, guys," Dad sang, and he hustled us out of the car. He bounded up the four stone steps to the porch.

As I passed through the blue door, a little sign burned into one of the logs caught my eye. It read: BUILT BY ABE LINCOLN LOG HOMES, UNICOI, TENNESSEE, 1995.

I stopped and touched the side of the building. It wasn't old at all. It was solid and freshly painted, and then some of the paint had been chipped off on purpose, to make it *look* old! I don't know why, Mud, but that really bugged me.

"Hello? Ivy? We're here!" my father called when we were all inside.

I looked around. The place was filled from floor to ceiling with stuff. One wall had a set of shelves overflowing with greeting cards, ceramic dogs, bird feeders, picture frames, refrigerator magnets, fancy soap, bath salts, teapots, oven mitts, flip-flops, and a whole section just for cookie jars shaped like school buses.

The opposite wall was covered with tablecloths and napkins, flower pots, watering cans, straw hats, fishing poles, and BB guns. A sign next to the guns said AMMO UP FRONT.

Down the middle aisle were snacks: Twinkies, Devil Dogs, chips, candy bars, fudge, crackers, and trail mix, right next to a bunch of gross stuff like pâté, sardines, bean dip, Spam, and smoked fish. Ew.

At the end of the aisle, next to the snack shelves, stood a bunch of wooden barrels labeled for fresh vegetables and fruit. They were all empty, except for one labeled APPLES and one labeled POTATOES that had onions in it.

Our father herded us over to the far end of the store, where there was a counter, a couple of beat-up old stools, and an old-timey chalkboard menu. Yeah, probably brand-spanking-new, from the Wal-Mart down the road.

"Ivy, have you been eaten by bears? Where the heck are you?" Dad hollered.

"No, no, I'll be right there!" she yelled from the basement.

Moments later she appeared, lugging a huge box of toilet paper. She dropped it on the floor and went over to give Dad a hug.

"Hello! Hello! I'm so glad you guys are here," she said to all of us.

Teddy and I kept a polite distance. But Ryan popped out from behind the snack shelves, ran over to her, and gave her a huge hug around the legs.

"Mooo merb," he said.

Ivy giggled. "What's he saying?" she asked me.

"I don't know," I lied.

She looked at me like she didn't believe me. But who cares?

She bent down to Ryan's level. "Hey, you want some ice cream?"

My little brother's eyes lit up like firecrackers and he clapped his hands together like a monkey.

"Let's see," Ivy said, stroking her chin. "I bet your

favorite flavor is mint chocolate chip. Am I right?"

"Glimble flerp." Ryan nodded, hopping up and down.

"Well, I make all the ice cream myself, and I do believe I have exactly what you need, my friend."

She offered Ryan her hand and hoisted him onto one of the beat-up old stools.

All I could think was *That's low, lady: buying my little brother's friendship with a dish of mint chocolate chip. Even if it is his favorite flavor.*

Ivy's red hair was in a bun with a black chopstick jabbed through it, and little wisps slipped out as she disappeared into the freezer once, twice, three times to scoop the ice cream. I don't like her very much, but I admit I liked what she was wearing: a big black sweater over a long gray flannel skirt with red tights, thick socks, and old work boots. And then I spied with my little eye the initials "T.M.C." on Ivy's sleeve. It wasn't her sweater at all. It was one that Gunda had knit for Dad. Can you believe that? I know cause she always embroidered Dad's initials on the cuff. Gee whiz, how low is Ivy going to go?

Right then I was ready to leave, and Teddy hadn't even unzipped his coat. Ugh. I wished I hadn't promised Dad I would try to be nice. I turned to Ivy and asked her sweetly, "Is this place yours?"

"Uh-huh." She smiled.

"Who's Esther?" I pointed over my shoulder. "The sign outside says, 'Esther's General Store.'"

Ivy laughed. "Oh, there is no Esther. I made it up. I thought it sounded like the perfect name for an old-fashioned country store. Don't you think?"

I think you're a moron!

As Ivy sprinkled jimmies on top of Ryan's ice cream, she turned to Dad and said quietly, "Theo, how did it go?"

"How did what go?!" snapped Teddy.

Ivy jumped a little and glanced from Teddy to Dad, like *Help!* "Um . . . well, your father was supposed to tell you guys—"

Dad interrupted. "I tried. I really tried, but it didn't go the way I planned. And then these two deer jumped out in front of us and I thought I was going to hit them and—"

"—And then he pulled over and started again, but we were way ahead of him. We guessed he was taking us to see *you*." Teddy gave Ivy the stink eye.

But she was *unfazed*. "And your father didn't mention anything else?" she asked calmly, looking in my direction.

"No,"I whispered. Oh boy, I wanted to be home with Green Bean.

Ivy squared off with Dad and put her hands on her hips in that I-mean-business way that Mom does. "You need to tell them, Theo. How about now?" She said it like it was an order, not a question.

"I will. Let's all just have some ice cream first," Dad suggested.

Teddy, Ivy, and I shouted, "No!"

Ryan, who was already up to his elbows in mint chip, stopped eating and held his spoon in the air like he'd been caught red-handed doing something he shouldn't.

Dad was irked now. "All right, everybody just settle down."

Teddy stepped forward. "Don't tell me to settle down. What is she talking about? What? Are you dumping Mom and marrying *her*?" My brother pointed to Ivy, who now turned red, then white as paper.

"You are out of line, Teddy," said Dad.

"But I'm right, aren't I?" he pushed.

"Not exactly. Like I said, change can be hard. But hear me out, because this one's going to be great, too." Dad took a deep breath and put on a smile. "Ivy and I have bought a bed-and-breakfast together."

Teddy and I looked at each other, confused, cause that didn't sound so bad.

Dad nervously continued, "It's in Cambridge, Massachusetts, which means I'll be looking to move up there within the year."

My heart climbed right into my throat, Mud. And it looked like Teddy stopped breathing.

"You're moving?" I said, choking on the words.

"Yes. But not for a while. And you guys will come visit us all the time."

Ryan covered his face with his sticky fingers and started to bawl.

"Does Mom know?" I asked.

"Yes, I told her the day before yesterday."

Teddy had fury in his eyes now. "You both knew and you waited until now to tell us? What's the matter with you?!" he bellowed. "This means you're getting a divorce, doesn't it?"

Ryan had crawled into Dad's arms and was sobbing into his shoulder. Our father looked down at the floor guiltily. "Well, we haven't made any final decisions, but yes, it looks like that's what's best."

"For who? You mean it's best for *you*!" shouted Teddy, and stormed out of the store.

In earth science class we read about this farmer who was struck by lightning. He said he didn't think it could happen to him and he never saw it coming. Said he was out in the rain, heard some distant thunder on his way to the barn, and then *WHAM!* He saw a flash of light, and the next thing he knew, he was zooming through the air. First he felt hot, then cold, then absolutely nothing.

When he came to, he realized that when he was struck, he'd been thrown fifteen feet.

Standing there, in pretend-Esther's General Store, I thought, *I know what you mean, Mister!*

Dad tried to hush Ryan and reach out to comfort me. But I wouldn't let him.

"Lorelei, are you okay?" he asked.

I shook my head no. I couldn't talk, Mud. Not cause I didn't have anything to say. But cause I had too much, and I was afraid of what might come out. I left and went outside to look for Teddy.

My brother was across the street at the edge of the clearing. He gazed out at the open field and the brick house with the tall white columns in the distance. It was snowing harder now, and Teddy's hair and down jacket were getting soaked. His face was wet too, from snowflakes and tears.

"Our father is a wad," he said bitterly.

"Yeah. I'd say *both* our parents are wads."

He looked at me sadly. "You know, I used to think we were so lucky to have a dad like ours. I remember before Ryan was born, before he worked all the time, he was funny and weird and always got excited about doing new things with us. But now I realize he doesn't care if he does those things *with* us or not. He's just going to do them, no matter what."

I hadn't thought of that, Mud. But Teddy was right.

My brother looked up at the gray sky and shook his wet head miserably. "Come on, let's get out of here," he grumbled.

We headed back to the store. Dad was already in the car with Ryan and about to come looking for us. All three of us sat in the backseat on the way home. Our father tried to explain for a while how things would be different but still great. That we would love Cambridge and he would see us all the time. But when he got no reply, he gave up and we drove the rest of the way in silence.

When we got home, Teddy carried Ryan straight upstairs to his room. I went into my room to hug Green Bean and be by myself. And Dad asked Mom to step outside for a minute where he could talk to her privately. I lay down on my bed, but I couldn't get my brain to shut up. I couldn't stop thinking about Dad moving to Cambridge.

I looked out my bedroom window at my parents standing in the driveway. Mom had the collar of her sweater with the roses on it pulled up around her ears, just listening. Dad talked a mile a minute, thumping his forehead with his fist. Probably saying, "I'm such a meathead. Today was a catastrophe!"

But let's face it, Mud. They both knew about him moving away, and neither one had the guts to tell us until we dragged it out of them. That makes them both meatheads.

Suddenly I didn't want to be by myself anymore. I grabbed Green Bean and a deck of cards and went down the hall to join my brothers in Teddy's room.

The three of us played go fish for a long time. Then Teddy got us some Cokes and we had a burping contest, which he won without even trying, of couse!

When it was dinnertime, Mom said she wasn't hungry and went to lie down. So I made my brothers and me grilled cheese sandwiches. We ate them in front of the TV (which Mom never lets us do!), and for a little while we forgot all about her and Dad and Ivy and everything that happened today.

It was just right.

Love,

Lorelei

⊘⁄⊘

1:16 A.M.

I can't sleep. I keep thinking maybe it's my fault that Dad is moving to Massachusetts. Maybe if I hadn't written that I don't miss him as much as I used to, he would stay. Not that I ever said those words out loud. But he must have figured it out somehow or he wouldn't be going.

Oh, Mud, what have I done?

Word of the Day: *forlorn (adj.): alone and unhappy.*
"With no one to play with, Rudolph the Red-nosed
Reindeer looked *forlorn*."

◎╱◎

Dear Mud,

Dad came over again. He wanted to talk to us kids
about yesterday. But when he drove up, Teddy refused
to see him and snuck out the back door. And Ryan was
already out with Mom, so it was just me.

I *wanted* to see him. I wanted to try to convince him
not to move away. Cause even though I wrote that I don't
miss him that much anymore, I only meant I'm getting
used to him not living with us. I was just being brave!
You know, in case he and Mom don't get back together.
Isn't that what I'm supposed to do?

Ugh, I'm confused.

Anyway, Dad didn't want to talk at the house. He
wanted to drive to the park, so I put on
my white furry earmuffs and matching
scarf and mittens that I got for Christmas
this year from Aunt Lee.

Yesterday's snow didn't stick very much in the city, but the park was still covered and looked really pretty. The weatherman said there's more snow on the way. I hope he's right for once.

It was too cold to sit on a bench, which was fine by me. I wanted to keep moving.

Dad started off our talk by saying he was sorry. "Things didn't go the way I planned yesterday. And I realize now, I should have broken the news to you guys in a different way. I apologize for that."

"It's okay," I said softly.

The wind picked up and made my eyes water.

"I wish your brothers were here," Dad said.

"Me too."

My father put his arm around me. "I want to explain what's going on as best I can, Peanut. I know there have been a lot of changes lately. Some of them scary. None of them easy. But I promise we'll get through them. The only thing you and your brothers have to remember is that your mother and I love you kids more each day, and we're enormously proud of you. The fact that we can't stay together as a couple has nothing to do with you guys. Not one thing. It's strictly between us."

"Okay, but I have to ask you something. Even if you and Mom split up, why do you have to move? Is it something we did? Something *I* did?"

"No, no. Stop right there." My father put his hands on my shoulders. "Now listen to me. Are you listening?"

"Yes," I whispered into the icy wind.

"This is not your fault. There is absolutely nothing you could have done, or should have done, to make this turn out differently. And it's not your brothers' fault either. This is between your mother and me. Period. Do you read me?"

Yes, I nodded. It felt like my tears were going to freeze to my eyelashes. We started walking again.

"I love you, Peanut." He tucked me under his arm. "You're a very brave, smart girl. I wish this wasn't so hard on you, but I have confidence that one day you and your brothers will understand why it's better for your mom and me to be apart."

"Okay," I said, cause I wanted to believe him, Mud. But the truth is, I couldn't imagine how that would be true. I felt so scared and tired, and terribly, terribly sad inside.

As we walked past the swings, Dad started to tell me about the bed-and-breakfast he and Ivy have bought. How great it is and blah, blah, blah. But it was like I was in this really long tunnel and could hardly hear him. All I could feel was the wind blowing right through me.

When we got home, Mom was there, so Dad didn't want to come in. I went straight upstairs. Through Teddy's door I could hear old rock and roll playing on his stereo, which is usually a sign that he doesn't want to be disturbed.

I knocked anyway.

My brother yanked open the door, and you'll never believe who was standing behind him, Mud. Matt Newsome!

"Yeah? What do you want?" snapped Teddy.

"Um . . . I'll come back later."

"It's okay, I gotta go anyway." Matt chuckled, then slapped my brother on the back. "Dude, we'll talk," he said.

As he slithered by, he lunged at me. "BOO!"

"Aaah!" I screamed, and almost fell on my butt.

Matt and Teddy howled with laughter and high-fived each other.

Very funny.

When Matt was out of sight, I turned to my brother.

"I didn't know you and Bonehead were friends. I thought you just did his homework for him."

"*Shush!* Matt's not a bad guy," Teddy said defensively.

I shook my head in disbelief.

"Can I come in?"

"Okay." Teddy turned down the music.

I climbed onto the bed and scooted back so I could lean against the wall.

"What did Dad say to you?"

"You know, all the usual stuff, like he and Mom love us, and that will never change."

My brother rolled his eyes.

"He said he and Mom can't live together anymore and that's one of the reasons he's moving to Massachusetts with Ivy. Oh, and he said one day we'll understand."

Teddy shook his head sadly. Then he whipped around and grabbed the *Life in Hell* mug off his desk that was full of pens and pencils, and hurled it against the wall. It broke, and pencils and pens scattered everywhere.

Yikes! I covered my head with my arms.

"What else did he say?" Teddy fumed.

"I don't know. I stopped listening after that," I squeaked, peeking at him between my fingers.

Teddy stood there panting. His hands balled up with fury. Then he looked over at me and hopped onto the bed. He reached out to me, but I jerked away cause I thought he was about to put me in a headlock or something, he still seemed so mad.

But he tugged on my sweatshirt and said, "No, no, come 'ere, little sister. I'm sorry I scared you. I'm sorry. I didn't mean to."

I lifted my head up slowly. *Is this my brother Teddy?* I thought. I let him put his arm around me.

"Listen, our parents may be crazy, but you and Ry and me have each other. No matter what happens. If Dad wants to go, I say, 'See ya later.' " Teddy saluted the air like a soldier. "Besides, it's way better than Mom and him staying together and fighting all the time. And if worse comes to worst, and Mom loses her Triscuits, I'll get a job and we'll go live with Aunt Lee. But we'll be together. That's a promise."

Like I said, I couldn't believe it was Teddy talking. It made me want to poke him in the head just to make sure it was him. Cause think about it, Mud: Yesterday he was furious at Dad. Furious! "Life sucks!" And now, right here beside me, he was Mr. Sunshine.

I said, "If everything's all fine and dandy, how come you refused to see Dad today?"

"Because he's still acting like a wad, and I don't feel like being nice to him."

That's Teddy for you.

I hugged him and went to my room.

I lay down on my bed next to Green Bean and stared at my Jennifer Aniston poster. Tears collected in my eyes cause something had been bugging me all afternoon, Mud, and I finally figured out what it was: Mom. What's going to happen to Mom without Dad around?

As in: Who will my brothers and I go to when she blows her lump about something? We need Dad to calm her down. He's the only one who knows how.

I cried into my pillow. Next thing I knew, Mom was knocking on my door.

"What's wrong?" she asked.

I couldn't tell her *everything*, so I just said, "I wish you and Dad weren't getting a divorce. And I wish he wasn't moving away."

Of course, she sat on my bed and held me tight and told me all the same things Dad did. That they love us kids to death and it doesn't matter if we live in the same house or not, we'll still be a family. Blah. Blah. I stopped listening cause hearing it again didn't make me feel any less *forlorn*.

That's when I decided if Mom and Dad are going to do whatever they want, I need to learn to take care of myself too. I'm not really sure how to do that, but I'm going to figure it out. Cause you never know what's going to happen, Mud. You just never know. And you don't want to be out in the world without your butter and eggs, as Grandpa used to say.

I miss you.

Love,

Lorelei xxoo

Word of the Day: *handily (adv.): skillfully; expertly; easily.*
"Curly Portis, the sixth-grade class clown, **handily** duped the teacher into sitting on a tack."

⦿⦿

Dear Mud,

Jenny called me from Texas this morning. Her uncle died. He was her dad's twin brother, so her dad's been bawling all morning. The good news is he probably won't move the family to Texas now that his brother's gone. The bad news is they still need a bigger house or Jenny will lose her mind sharing a room with three of her sisters.

Guess what else happened today. Mom dropped me, Teddy, and Ryan off at the mall, and we saw Bo! Why, oh why, did I have to be there with my smelly brothers? At least Bo was there with his mom and grandmother, who

 came all the way from England to spend Christmas with them. She has a pretty English accent like Bo's mom and, for a grandma, hardly any wrinkles.

I *handily* ditched Ryan and Teddy at the toy store, so Bo and I could chat for a second.

"What did you get for Christmas?" he asked.

"Stuff." I shrugged. "How 'bout you?"

"Same." He smiled.

"How long is your grandma visiting?"

"Three weeks." And he made a face that let me know he thought that was way too long.

"Don't you like her?" I laughed.

"She's okay. She just treats me like a baby. She's always fixing my hair or telling me to eat this, eat that. I keep saying, 'Nanna, I'm eleven! I can take care of myself.' But she never wants to let me out of her sight."

And before I could stop myself, I blurted out, "Gee whiz, you should come over to my house; nobody's watching us!"

I know! What is wrong with me, Mud? I clapped my hand over my mouth and turned bright red.

But Bo laughed and said, "That'd be fun."

I thought I would die, Mud. *Die of happiness, that is!* A minute later his mom and grandma came to collect him. As they approached, his nanna licked her thumb and wiped something invisible off his face. Bo looked at me, like *See what I mean?* It made me smile.

I ran into the toy store and found my brothers.

"How's your boyfriend?" Teddy said, and flicked me in the head.

"He is not my boyfriend, but we've got to tell Mom to get some furniture, and *fast*!"

Your totally excited pal,

Lorelei

XOXOXOXOXO

Saturday, December 31st

Word of the Day: *fruitful (adj.): producing good results.*
"Bartering with Mr. Fogg at the garden store turned out to be extremely *fruitful.*"

◎╱◎

Dear Mud,

It's New Year's Eve, so I thought I'd write down some New Year's resolutions. That's what grown-ups do. They write down a list of things they want to accomplish over the coming year. As though writing them down will make it easier to do them. Not. My mom's list never changes.

She always has "lose weight" (even though she doesn't need to), "join a gym" (even though she hates being sweaty), "be better about being on time" (never going to happen), and my favorite: "try out for the US Olympic diving team." Yeah, right. She's a really good swimmer, but she's afraid of heights.

Dad has a list also. It only has two things on it: 1. Work less. 2. Play more.

Mom says he's the only person

337

she's ever known who has accomplished everything on his list.

So I was thinking, if I'm going to start being more independent, I ought to have a list too.

Here it is (in no particular order):

1) Get a job or start my own business.
2) Learn to cook more than Pop-Tarts and grilled cheese.
3) Spend more time playing with Green Bean.
4) Kiss a boy. (You know who!)
5) Do ten things that scare me before my twelfth birthday.
6) Keep writing my life's story.

Mom's having a New Year's Eve party downstairs. She wasn't going to cause we hardly have any furniture, but she decided that didn't matter in the end.

"It's the people who make the party, right?" she said.

Sure, if you like people who turn your living room into a zoo. It sounds like the monkey house down there; everybody laughing and howling over the music, and nobody more than Mom.

We kids aren't invited to these parties. Which means Teddy went out who knows where. Ryan is spending the night at Mrs. Bixley's, and Green Bean and I are snug in my bed. Snug and writing to you, watching the snow fall outside my window.

All day I've been thinking about everything that's happened in the past two and a half months. You died, I started keeping this diary, I became a celebrity at school, and my parents split up—to name four! Four gargantuan things I never even thought about before October 15th. It sure makes me wonder (and worry a little) about what next year will bring.

The good thing is, I'm going to be twelve on my next birthday, which is pretty mature. Poor little Ryan's only going to be five. There's still a lot of stuff that makes you cry when you're five. Luckily, he has Teddy and me. And he's sure going to need us when Dad moves away.

Well, it's two minutes to midnight, Mud. Happy New Year! And thank you, with all my heart, for always being there for me. It's funny how you did that even though you're dead.

More later.

Love and hugs and smooches,

Lorelei xo

Acknowledgements

In the world, people like to refer to your artistic endeavor as "your baby." "How's your baby coming along?" they say.

She's good, thanks. But I am honor bound to heap gratitude on the village that helped me raise her.

Thank you to Claudette Sutherland, teacher extraordinaire, of the Tuesday night writing class where *I, Lorelei* was born and became a proper book. How stellar of you to create that space. As well, hugs and thanks to Kathy Miller Kelley, who sat across from me each week and asked the most illuminating questions.

Jim McCarthy, my book agent, who totally gets it.

Laura Geringer and Jill Santopolo, who graciously took Lorelei in and gave her a home.

Renée Cafiero, senior production editor, who circled every single "so" in the third draft. Oy! You made me a better writer.

Lee Wildish for charming, witty illustrations.

And finally, love and thanks to Daniel Erickson, who read it and read it and read it. You always said, "You're exactly where you're supposed to be. . . ."

You were always right.

YS
Fall 2008
Los Angeles, California